All That Summer Left

Ayla Ali

First Edition, 2025
All That Summer Left
Written by Ayla Ali

For Zaki - May your legacy remain.

Part One

Emma

The last bell of the year rang out across the school like a starting pistol, sharp and piercing, slicing through the heavy air. The familiar clang of metal on metal echoed down the corridors, mixing with the distant hum of voices that quickly swelled into a roar. The scent of fresh-cut grass drifted through the open windows, mingling with the warm hint of early summer sunshine, softening the sharp edges of the school's concrete and brick. There was also that unmistakable, slightly musty smell of lockers left unopened for days, an odd combination of sweat, old books, and faint traces of forgotten lunches. It all seemed to hold the memories of seven years, compressed into one last breath.

The noise erupted like a wave. Shouts of jubilation, laughter bubbling and spilling over, feet pounding the floor in wild rhythms, and the slam of lockers closing one after another created a chaotic symphony. Hands were thrown into the air, some waving wildly in excitement, others grasping balloons that bounced in the sudden surge of movement. A few balloons slipped free, drifting lazily upwards as if reluctant to leave. A stray piece of confetti, small and shimmering, floated down like a tiny snowflake caught in the turmoil. Students jostled each other, shoulders bumping, as they surged forward, carried on a current of relief and exhilaration that had been building all year.

I stood just outside the main doors, on the front steps, where the rush was a little less wild but still electrifying. Lily was at my side, silent, her hands folded tightly in front of her, her eyes watching the tide of students spilling out of the sixth-form building like a hive breaking apart. The energy around us was a storm, unstoppable and roaring but Lily seemed untouched by it, a quiet island in a sea of noise. This was the moment we had waited for and dreaded in equal measure. The end of our A-levels, the end of school, the end of everything we had known and built together over seven years.

I thought about the future waiting just beyond the horizon, Manchester University in the autumn, a fresh start, a new chapter. I still remember the exact moment I became obsessed with human behaviour. I must have been about ten. Mum had picked me up late from a school club, and we stopped at a petrol station on the way home. There was a man at the till, tall, neatly dressed, with a warm smile but I noticed his hands were trembling as he paid, and he kept glancing at the security mirror in the corner. Something about him didn't match. Everyone else seemed oblivious, but I couldn't stop watching him. He left quickly, and five minutes later, a staff member came running out saying someone had taken a wallet from the counter. I remember turning to Mum and saying, "It was the man in the navy coat," and the look she gave me, half impressed, half unsettled, has stuck with me ever since.

Since then, I'd learned to read people's tells. Micro-expressions, body language, tone shifts. Not always

perfect, of course, but I liked to believe I had a sense for what simmered underneath. The stories people didn't say aloud. It made the world make more sense to me. Safer, somehow. Like if I could understand people, I could prepare myself for what might come next.

Psychology was the only path I could see for myself; I had always been drawn to understanding what made people tick, fascinated by the hidden motives behind their actions and the emotions they barely spoke aloud. I liked to think I was a good judge of character, someone who could read between the lines of people's smiles and silences. Yet, standing here now amid the cacophony, I realised how little I truly understood about the emotions swirling inside me, and inside Lily.

Her stillness spoke louder than the crowd around us. While everyone else was shouting and cheering, she seemed to carry a quiet weight, something unspoken pressing down beneath her calm exterior. I wanted to reach out, to break through the bubble of noise and confusion, but words caught in my throat. The wild celebration felt so far away from the subdued storm inside her eyes.

The summer warmth wrapped around us, a stark contrast to the chill in my chest. I could almost taste the bittersweet mix of endings and beginnings hanging thick in the air. This was more than just the last day of school. It was a farewell to a chapter of our lives written in laughter, tears, friendship, and growth. And while the crowd surged forward like a wave, carrying everyone toward the future, I wondered how many of us were really ready to ride it.

Ben and Maya sprinted toward us, faces bright with excitement, arms thrown around our shoulders.Tom followed, carrying a speaker blasting music, already planning where the first party of summer would be.

We weren't the most popular group at St. Cedars Sixth Form at least, that's how some people might put it. Of course, popularity is such a slippery thing; it depends entirely on who you ask. We weren't the ones throwing wild parties every weekend or racking up every sports trophy in the school cabinet. We didn't dominate the headline gossip or take over the hottest tables in the cafeteria. But somehow, everyone knew us. Everyone liked us. We were the kind of group who belonged everywhere but nowhere in particular, slipping seamlessly between cliques without stepping on toes or stirring drama. Invitations came without us needing to ask, whether it was to a study session, a casual movie night, or a last-minute hangout after school.

I think it all boiled down to one thing: we were easygoing and genuine. There was no pretence, no trying to prove something we weren't. We made people feel welcome, like there was always room for one more in the conversation or the circle. Maybe that was why even the most unlikely of friends could find common ground with us.

I'd say I was the natural leader of the group, not because I bossed anyone around or demanded attention, but because I carried the kind of optimism that made people lean in.

I'm the one who always believed the best moments were just waiting around the corner, like they were hiding behind the next door, ready to surprise us. I guess it's hard to resist someone who sees the silver lining in the gloomiest of days. Always beside me is my twin, Lily, identical in looks with those same glinting green eyes and the easy smile that could soften any mood. But where I'm loud and optimistic, Lily is quiet and thoughtful. She's happiest tucked away with a sketchpad in her lap and a pencil behind her ear, drawing the world as she sees it, one delicate line at a time. There's something calming about her presence, like a gentle anchor that steadies me when my thoughts start to race. She has this way of warming up any room she's in, her quiet strength and calm logic balancing out my sometimes irrational bursts of excitement.

Then there's Tom Grant, the joker of the group. Quick with a grin and a sharp wit, Tom always knows how to light up a room. He's got a knack for telling stories that have everyone laughing so hard they forget what they were worried about just moments before. There's an effortless charm about him, he can get people to listen without even trying. Honestly, it's no surprise that everyone seems to have a crush on him; I don't blame them. Even when he's just tossing out a cheeky comment or flashing that cheeky smile, you can tell he's the kind of person who brightens your day without you realising it. His girlfriend, Maya Brooks, is the perfect foil to him. Sharp-witted and fiercely loyal, she's the one who cuts through the noise when things get too messy or complicated. Maya has this steady, fierce energy, like a quiet storm that makes people feel safe just being near her. She's not flashy, but she's unforgettable.

And then there's Ben Carter, shy, bookish, the quiet heart of the group. You'll usually find him with a novel half-read sticking out of his backpack or tucked under his arm. Ben's kindness is gentle but firm; he's the one who listens when the others get too loud, who notices the things others miss. Even though he sometimes hangs back, he's never left behind. There's a depth to him that grows on you, like a secret melody you want to learn by heart.

This is the crew, the patchwork family I've known for so long that it's hard to remember what life was like before we became this stitched-together unit. We're bound by late-night phone calls, shared secrets whispered in the dark, endless inside jokes that no one else understands, and memories that blur together into one long, golden haze. We've been through it all, laughter and heartbreak, silly arguments and moments of quiet understanding and somehow, we keep coming back to each other. No matter where life takes us next, this group is home.

"You ready for the best summer ever?" Maya grinned, already pulling out a crumpled list she'd made, beach trips, late-night walks, bonfires, all the clichés we swore we'd do before university tore us in different directions.I laughed, letting the buzz sweep me up, but beside me, Lily stayed quiet.

I couldn't help but notice how tired her eyes looked. Her smile didn't reach her eyes. Her arms hung loosely at her sides while the rest of us clutched each other, laughing at jokes we'd told a thousand times. She's my best friend and I don't know what I'm going to do living away from her. Today, she seemed even further away.

"You okay?" I asked quietly, nudging her with my elbow.

She nodded too quickly. "Yeah. Just... feels weird, doesn't it?"

"Weird good," I said. "Come on, Lily. We made it."

She smiled again, but it wavered at the edges.

Looking around at the crowds, the people shouting promises to stay in touch, even though we all knew most of them would be broken by October. I suddenly understood. It was weird. We'd spent years dreaming about the end, about finally being free of homework and uniforms and teachers who didn't listen. But now that it was here, it felt hollow. Like something we hadn't realised we'd miss until it was already slipping away.

I threw an arm around her shoulders. "Hey. We've got all summer, right? We'll make it unforgettable."

Lily nodded again, her gaze drifting back to the others. A shadow of anxiety crossed her face before she pulled herself together.

"Yeah," she said softly. "Unforgettable."

"Lil, talk to me. You've been weird for weeks, this is the time of our lives, what's going on?"

Lily turned to face Emma, eyes so wide you could see the hints of hazel against her green iris.

"You know you mentioned a few days ago that you felt like something weird was going to happen, like you were being watched?, I feel it too" She says with a quiver in her voice.

Suddenly I could feel the weight of every useless textbook in my bag, this same feeling I'd been having for weeks. Lily was sensing it too, but I couldn't let my sister think anything was wrong. I'm the tough one, I always have been, I'll deal with this for us both. I have to protect Lily.

I turned back to Lily,

"The twin telepathy is doing its thing again! Look Lil it's nothing, remember what we learnt about? How twins are so connected that sometimes they can't separate the fact from fiction? Well here it is so cheer up, we're about to have the best summer ever!"

Lily smiled, a huge wide eye smile, knowing she'd believed every word. As we gathered our bags and walked toward the car park, I felt it for the first time: A ripple in the summer heat. A tiny shiver against my skin. Someone, somewhere, was watching. I'd been feeling this for weeks. It's probably just my end of year, new life anxiety.

When I turned, there was only the school behind us, old bricks glowing gold in the afternoon light, windows dark and empty. I shook it off. We had adventures to plan. We had memories to make.

We had no idea what was already waiting for us, hidden just beyond the edges of what we could see.

2

DI Tee / DC Zak

The inside of the car smelled like lukewarm fries and stale coffee.

At first glance, Detective Inspector Theodora "Tee" Lang didn't look like your typical detective. She was young, younger than most expected for someone in her position and stood just a shade over five feet tall, with a lean frame that made people mistake her for a civilian more often than not. Her sharp, ice-blue eyes were usually the first thing that gave her away. They missed nothing. They darted from face to detail to pattern with relentless focus, constantly assembling a picture no one else could see. Tee's face was delicate, almost elfin, the kind people underestimated far too easily but there was a steel beneath her calm exterior that stopped people in their tracks once they saw her in action.

Anyone who knew her knew better than to judge by appearances. She was fierce, unapologetically direct, and dryly funny when the situation allowed. Tee didn't posture or throw her weight around, she didn't need to. She let her work speak for itself. Top of her class at Hendon Police College, she had a natural, almost eerie intuition for investigative work. While others followed procedure like a checklist, Tee followed threads that most couldn't even see. She trusted her gut more than she trusted people, not because she was jaded, but because her instincts had rarely failed her.

She had a knack for spotting the details that slipped through the cracks, the slight hesitation in a voice, the misplaced smudge of mud on a clean floor, a gesture repeated one time too many. She approached crime scenes like abstract art: never head-on, but from the side, where the shadows sharpened and the truth could be teased out in the negative space. For Tee, solving a case wasn't about brute force or dramatic confessions, it was about precision. Quiet observation. Strategic pressure. And always staying ten steps ahead.

Beside her on the bench, Detective Constable Zak Ali was having a small battle with a quarter-pounder that he was determined not to drop all over his lap. He was cradling it on his knee, wrestling the paper wrapper open with the delicate care of someone diffusing a bomb. Ketchup oozed precariously close to his white shirt, and he was holding his breath like that might somehow keep gravity at bay.

Zak didn't look like the kind of guy who'd chase down suspects in alleyways or confront killers in an interview room. He had a wiry, almost academic build, more university lecturer than law enforcement officer. His black curls were a perpetual mess, like he'd run his hands through them too many times while thinking, and his wire-rimmed glasses were always slipping down the bridge of his nose, no matter how many times he pushed them back up. His sleeves were rolled halfway up his forearms in a permanent gesture of readiness, even if the rest of him gave off a slightly distracted, bookish vibe.

But Tee knew better. Zak was one of the sharpest minds she'd ever worked with and not just intellectually. He had a kind of emotional fluency that made him invaluable in the field. He understood people deeply, instinctively and had an almost unnerving talent for making suspects feel safe enough to talk, sometimes without even realising they were revealing anything. He could disarm with a well-placed question or a patient silence, drawing out confessions like threads from fabric. Where Tee spotted the cracks in a story, Zak could feel the shifts in tone, the tremor in a voice, the emotions rippling just beneath the surface.

Together, they balanced each other, the sharp edge and the soft probe, the blade and the balm. While others chased answers with noise and force, Tee and Zak worked in quiet synchrony, unpicking the truth with patience and precision. No flash. No bravado. Just results.

Tee always said: *If you wanted to kick a door down, send me. If you wanted a soul cracked open, send Zak.*

Together, they were a force few could reckon with brains, guts, instinct and heart, all tangled up into a partnership that had, somehow, survived three years of impossible cases.

"You ever think," Zak said swallowing his burger, "that if we just stayed parked here all day, pretending to be busy, nobody would notice?"

Tee shot him a sideways look, her mouth curling into the faintest smirk.

"In this town?" she said. "Someone would notice. Then they'd write a letter to the council saying we're wasting taxpayer money."

Zak chuckled, brushing salt from his fingers onto his jeans.

Outside, the summer heat pressed against the windows, blurring the edges of the world.
It was the kind of thick, syrupy evening that made even the most restless parts of town feel sleepy and harmless, like violence couldn't possibly happen in heat like this. The radio crackled sharply, snapping both of them upright.

"Unit 4-9, possible animal disturbance. Multiple reports, Cedar Lane. Request attendance."

Tee sighed.

Animal disturbance. Probably a fox getting into bins. Nothing to get excited about.

Zak reached lazily for the radio, licking ketchup from his thumb as he clicked it on.

"Unit 4-9 attending," he said.

Tee shoved the keys into the ignition, and the engine rumbled to life. The McDonald's wrappers in the back shifted with a crinkling noise. As they pulled away from the car park, Tee glanced sideways at Zak.

The sun was sliding lower now, bleeding orange across the rows of houses and shops, turning the town into a shadow-play of gold and black. It felt like just another call, something small, something forgettable. Neither of them knew, not yet, that Cedar Lane was the beginning. That something much darker was about to claw its way into their lives.

The Cedar Lane estate was the kind of place where time had stalled somewhere around 1998 and never bothered catching up. The cul-de-sacs wound gently like coiled ribbons, the roads all looping back on themselves as if trying to keep their secrets close. Every street looked like a photocopy of the last, semi-detached homes with pebbledash fronts, faded hanging baskets, and the same brand of weather-stained patio furniture resting out back like forgotten guests at a garden party.

There was a uniformity to everything: matching white fences, lawns trimmed to regulation height, neat rows of bins tucked in at perfect angles. Even the cars looked rehearsed a lineup of sensible hatchbacks and lease-plan SUVs parked identically on identical driveways. Every window framed a life that looked pleasant enough from a distance. Smiling school photos on the walls. Scented candles flickering behind net curtains. The kind of place where the worst thing you'd expect to happen was a missed Amazon parcel or a passive-aggressive note about hedges creeping over property lines.

Nothing truly bad ever seemed to happen here. Or if it did, it happened quietly, behind closed doors and drawn blinds, where no one had to see it, and no one had to say anything. The air felt heavy with a strange stillness, like it had been holding its breath for years.

As the unmarked police car rolled down the main road, its flashing blue lights briefly lit up the estate like a warning flare. Curtains twitched, fingers parted slats in the blinds, faces flickered behind glass. But no one came outside. No one stepped onto their porches or leaned over their fences. This wasn't the kind of neighbourhood where people liked to get involved. Not directly. Not when things turned ugly.

People here preferred their tragedies neat and contained, whispered about over garden walls or dissected in WhatsApp groups under the guise of concern. The presence of law enforcement disrupted the delicate illusion

21

they all maintained, that everything was fine, that nothing truly dark could grow in places so carefully curated.

But Tee could feel it. Beneath the perfect lawns and picture frames, there was something else here. Something that had been rotting quietly for a while. You just had to know where to look and more importantly, how.

Tee killed the engine and stepped out, the thick, baked air clinging to her like a second skin.

Zak followed, scanning the neat driveways and potted plants with a slight frown. His burger was forgotten now, cooling on the passenger seat. The call had come from Number 23, a pensioner named Mrs. Whitby. She was standing at her gate when they approached, a trembling silhouette against the drooping hydrangeas.

"In the alleyway," she said, voice trembling. "Behind the bins… I didn't want to go closer."

"Good instinct," Tee muttered, giving the woman a tight smile.

She and Zak ducked down the narrow alley between two houses, the world narrowing around them into shadows and sour air. The scent hit them halfway down, metallic, sharp, wrong. Zak gagged softly, covering his nose with his sleeve. At the end of the alley, tucked behind the bins, something white caught the last slant of sunlight. Tee approached carefully, crouching low. It was a cat. Or at least, it had been.

Now it was a shattered, bloodied thing, its fur matted with something dark and sticky, almost like tar. The body had been mutilated with chilling precision, not just hurt, but *arranged,* in a way that was almost ritualistic.

Tee felt her stomach turn, but she kept her face blank. Zak hovered behind her, frozen for a moment, then exhaled sharply.

"Third one in a month," he said, his voice strained. "That we know about."

"More," Tee said grimly, standing up. "Most people don't report dead cats. Not unless it's like this."

They both stared down at the body, the alley closing in around them with its stifling heat and shadows.

Finally, Zak said, low, "You ever watch that Netflix thing, *Don't F** With Cats*?*"

Tee gave a humourless smile. "Unfortunately."

Zak nudged his glasses up his nose, the lenses catching the fading light.

"You remember how it started there? Small. Anonymous. Cruel."

"And then people died," Tee finished, voice flat.

Her mouth tightened as she looked down again, feeling the knot of unease twist tighter in her gut. They had been trying not to see it for weeks now. Trying to convince themselves that the scattered reports were just coincidence. Kids being cruel. Bad accidents. Nothing... organised. But standing here now, Tee knew better. Someone wasn't just killing animals.

They were practicing. Perfecting. Preparing. And worse, they were getting better at it.

Zak ran a hand through his hair, leaving it even more chaotic than before.

"You think we should…" he hesitated. "Start a file? Link the other ones officially?"

Tee nodded, once, sharp. "We should have started it two incidents ago."

Zak exhaled slowly. "You're thinking what I'm thinking, aren't you?"

"Yeah," Tee said. "I'm thinking escalation."

They both knew the pattern. They both knew how it went. First animals. Then something bigger. Something human.

She crouched again, scanning the scene, noting the details without touching anything. The clean cuts. The way the body was *posed,* almost like a doll discarded after a game.

No blood trail leading in, meaning the cat had been killed somewhere else, then brought here. Meaning planning. Meaning intent.

"Call it in," she said to Zak, voice steady but low. "Get forensics. Now."

Zak was already moving, muttering into his radio, his face grim.

Tee straightened up, dusting her hands on her jeans. Somewhere beyond the alley, the faint sound of children laughing floated on the warm evening air. It sounded wrong now. Mocking.

"We need to dig deeper," Tee muttered, half to herself. "This isn't just random violence. Someone's planning this."

Her mind was already racing, through every CCTV camera on Cedar Lane, through every scrap of witness statement they'd taken in the last six weeks and filed away under *probably nothing*. And she was willing to bet, willing to *swear* that whoever had done this was getting bolder. Practicing for something worse.

As the sun sank below the rooftops, throwing long shadows across the manicured lawns, Tee stood in that narrow alley and felt something shift. Something small, but irreversible. As if the town itself was holding its breath. Waiting. Waiting for the first real scream. Waiting for the first body. And somewhere, Tee thought, someone else was waiting too.

Smiling in the dark.
Planning their next move.

3

From the cracked attic window of Number 25 Cedar Lane, one house down from the commotion, I watched. Hidden. Still. Breathing shallow. My heart was beating, yes, but no longer racing. Not like before.

Below, in the alleyway, the two detectives crouched over what was left of my latest offering. The blonde one, sharp-eyed, quick to move, barked something into her radio. The man beside her looked softer, more uncertain. He fiddled with his glasses and cast nervous glances toward the shadows. They were alert. Observant. But not enough. The attic was thick with the smell of old things dust, mildew, rotting beams, but I found comfort in the stillness. I didn't mind the heat. Or the tightness in my chest. Because this time, there was something else rising to the surface.

Relief.

The alley cat, its body posed with care, limbs arranged like a ritual, had become something more than a statement. It was a release. A pressure valve turned. A weight lifted. A piece of art. No one would understand the calm that came after. They'd call it cruelty. Madness, maybe. But they'd be wrong. This wasn't about sadism. I didn't care about causing pain. It was about letting go. About not drowning under everything I'd been forced to carry. The laughter behind my back. The whispers in corridors. The isolation.

Emma. Maya. Tom. Ben. Lily.

Emma, always Emma, shining so brightly she never noticed the shadows she cast. They all looked the other way. Especially when the teasing got sharper. When "just a laugh" turned into silence. When lunch breaks became moments spent locked in bathroom stalls, waiting for it to end.

But the silence didn't matter anymore.

Not now.

The cats had become sacred. Ritualistic, not in the way the detectives would think. This wasn't about devils or symbols. It was quieter than that. Simpler. Every body had taken something from me. A grudge. A scar. A quiet scream.

And afterward? The stillness inside me was breathtaking. It started small. A spider. Its legs twitching as I watched. Then a bird, half-dead in the gutter. Then a rabbit. That one was hard. Messy. But afterward came the peace. Then the cats.

They were perfect. Soft. Beautiful. The first one was a stray. Alone. I cradled it afterward, whispering apologies through my tears. But the next came easier. And the next. Until now… the guilt was gone. In its place, there was calm. Not joy. Not happiness. Just a kind of peace, like standing in a room where no one expected me to smile.

The blonde detective looked up then, eyes scanning the rooftops. For a breath, our gazes almost met. I held my breath, not in fear, but in stillness. The way a deer freezes just before it bolts.

But the moment passed. She looked away. Dismissed. Not a threat. Not yet.

I leaned back from the window. My breath slowed again. My body quiet. Whole. I thought of them again, the ones who laughed the loudest. Who kept laughing, even when the cracks beneath them spread. They didn't know what was coming. Not death, I'd never wanted that. That was never the point.

It was truth I wanted. Exposure. Let them believe the killer was out there, stalking them. Let them panic. But I knew my limits. I never hurt people. Never wanted to. All I ever wanted was to feel something.

Or maybe… to feel nothing at all.

I've been invisible for so long. The one no one saw. Not even when I broke. Not even when I screamed, quietly, into pillowcases night after night.

Only one person had ever really seen me. Kind. Gentle. Understanding. Not like the teachers. Not like my family. Not like the ones who smiled at you in the halls and forgot you the moment the bell rang.

The person listened, said it was okay to feel everything. That feelings were heavy, sometimes too heavy to carry alone. That it was alright to let them go. And that first night, after our first conversation, that was when I found the dead mouse behind the bin, I didn't throw it away. I picked it up. Held it. Buried it myself.

That was the beginning.

Each time I laid out a new body, quiet, careful, waiting to be found. I wasn't proud. I wasn't thrilled. But afterward, my chest didn't feel crushed under the weight of everything I wasn't allowed to say. I didn't need forgiveness. I didn't need permission. I just needed space. And no one ever gave it to me.

So I took it, in fur and bone and silence.

Outside, the scene buzzed with noise. Officers moving. Neighbours whispering. The news would spread, another cat, another mystery. Talk of darkness. Of evil. But evil's just a story people tell to make the truth easier to swallow.

This wasn't evil. This was necessity.

I wiped the fog from the glass and took one last look. The detectives were pulling back. The yellow tape shimmered in the last of the evening light, drawn taut like the closing of something. Or maybe... the opening. I thought of Emma again, probably laughing. Planning the next perfect summer day. Plotting who to ruin next.

But she wouldn't laugh forever. I didn't want her to suffer… yet. I just wanted her to understand.

To know what it meant to be lonely.

To carry pain like a second skin.

To wake up and choose not to scream.

Just once, I wanted them all to see the world the way I saw it. Not broken. Just tilted. Off-kilter enough that every step felt like a fight for balance. I slipped back into the shadows of the attic. The glass stopped fogging. They'd never know my name. The police wouldn't see me coming. The town would whisper. The parents would panic. But I had never felt more clear. More certain. More alive.

Not because I killed.

But because, finally—

I could breathe.

4

Emma

The quarry lay just beyond the outskirts of town, a hidden gem carved out of the earth like a scar frozen in time. Once a bustling site of industry, its steep rock faces now stood silent, their jagged edges softened by creeping moss and wildflowers. The air carried a faint, mineral tang mixed with the fresh scent of pine and damp earth from the surrounding woods.

A narrow dirt path wound through thickets of brambles and tall grasses, leading to a wide, flat clearing near the water's edge. The quarry's heart was a deep, turquoise pool, still and glassy, reflecting the sky like a mirror broken only by the occasional ripple of a breeze or a daring bird's splash.

Around the pool, large flat stones and fallen logs formed natural seats, perfect for long conversations or quiet contemplation. Sunlight filtered through gaps in the trees, casting dappled patterns across the rocks, while dragonflies darted in lazy circles above the water's surface.

Despite its ruggedness, the quarry felt like a sanctuary, a place removed from the noise and judgment of the world.

Here, the group had shared laughter and secrets, plans and fears, their voices echoing softly off the cliffs.

At dusk, the quarry transformed. Shadows lengthened, the air cooled, and the sky blushed pink and orange, melting into twilight. Fires were sometimes lit in a small ring of stones, their warm glow flickering against the cold rock faces. The crackle of flames and the smell of woodsmoke mingled with whispered conversations and quiet songs.

It was their refuge, wild, untamed, yet strangely comforting. A place where they could be themselves, if only for a little while.

It was perfect.

Emma grinned as she helped unload the battered portable speakers from Ben's boot, dust puffing around their feet as they clambered down the worn track to the open ground. The sun was just beginning to sag toward the horizon, staining everything in bruised pinks and lazy golds. A few early arrivers, kids from the year below mostly, were already sitting cross-legged in the grass, talking too loudly, laughing at nothing.

This was it. The last summer. The last hurrah before they scattered like seeds on the wind, different cities, different futures.

And tonight, none of that mattered. Tonight was for them.

"Oi, careful!" Tom yelped as Maya nearly tripped over the tangled extension cable.

"You're the one who packed it like a lunatic," she shot back, tossing her dark curls over her shoulder and flashing him a teasing glare.

Emma shook her head fondly. Those two, chaos wrapped in skin.

Emma's gaze caught on her twin, trailing a few steps behind the group, hugging a worn denim jacket tight around herself despite the heat. Emma frowned slightly. Lily had been quiet all afternoon. Not sulky or angry. Just... sad. She kicked at a clump of dandelions, head down, hair slipping forward to shield her face. Emma's stomach twisted. She knew Lily struggled sometimes with the noise, the crowds. And tonight was a reminder of everything that was ending.

Emma knew Lily was scared, we just found out there was another cat found. Lily is sensitive and she's been going on about how cat killings turn into serial killers. We've all been thinking about it, but Lily internalises everything, this is really playing on her mind. This can't stop us from having the best summer.

Emma started toward her, but before she could reach her, someone yelled her name and the moment snapped.

*

33

The party bloomed around them like wildflowers, fast, messy, vibrant. Someone started up the speakers, and music blasted out over the quarry walls, bouncing and breaking into strange echoes. The little groups grew, split, reformed. Someone lit sparklers, the bright chemical fizz lighting up grinning faces and spinning shadows. Emma spun with it all, laughing until her ribs hurt, hugging people she barely knew, shouting promises of "We'll definitely visit!" that everyone knew were lies.

As the fire crackled and the night deepened, the group grew more animated, buoyed by a mix of nostalgia and hopeful anticipation for the future. Somewhere between laughter and music, someone, Ben, maybe stood up on a flat stone, raising his voice over the crackling flames.

"Okay, promise me this," he called out, eyes shining with a mix of mischief and sincerity. "No matter where uni takes us, we're coming back here. We visit. We don't let this end."

The circle hushed for a beat, then Maya stood, voice ringing clear through the night. "Absolutely. I'm holding you all to that."

One by one, the others shouted their own promises, "I'll visit!" "We're a team!" "No matter what!", their voices echoing off the quarry walls, carried by the cool night air.

Emma laughed despite herself, the sound mingling with the others, a fragile thread of connection woven through the darkness. Even Lily, sitting apart, allowed a small smile to curl at the corner of her lips, though her eyes seemed far away, lost in thoughts no one else could reach.

The quarry glowed in the falling dark. The air was thick with dust, smoke, and the hot metallic scent of summer. Everything felt bigger, louder, brighter. Like they could stay suspended here forever if they just held on tight enough.

Those promises, shouted into the open air, felt like a pact, fragile but fiercely held a vow to remain part of each other's lives, no matter the miles or challenges that lay ahead.

The quarry held their voices like a sacred trust, cradling their hopes against the vast sky, a fleeting moment of unity before the shadows began to close in.

Later, after the sun had fully slipped away and the stars bled into view, Emma found herself sitting on the hood of Tom's car, legs swinging, a sticky half-finished drink beside her. Tom was holding court nearby, cracking jokes, his arm draped lazily over Maya's shoulders. She leaned into him but her eyes kept flickering to Emma, sharp, assessing. Ben sat cross-legged at Emma's feet, babbling about some podcast he thought she'd love, cheeks pink with earnestness. Emma smiled and nodded and let his words wash over her without really listening.

Suddenly, chill scraped down Emma's spine. She slid off the car and made her way over to Lily, her trainers crunching quietly over the dirt.

"Hey," she said, trying for casual. "You alright?"

Lily blinked up at her, startled. Her face was shadowed, unreadable.

"Yeah," she said. Too quickly.

Emma sat down beside her, letting the silence stretch. The woods beyond the quarry rustled softly. An owl hooted, long and low.Emma bumped Lily's shoulder with hers.

"You know," she said lightly, "you could try pretending to have fun. Just once."

Lily's mouth twisted not quite a smile.

"I am," she said. "Its just, I can't shake that feeling."

She opened her mouth to say something else, something real, but then a group of boys whooped and someone set off a Roman candle, sending green sparks screaming into the sky. The moment shattered. Lily was already standing, brushing dust from her jeans.

"I'm gonna grab some water," she said,

Before Emma could respond, Lily was swallowed back into the crowd.

Hours bled together. The party grew looser, sloppier. Someone started a game of spin the bottle that quickly dissolved into chaos. A fight nearly broke out over a speaker cable. Someone else dared Tom to climb a half-collapsed fence. Emma wandered between groups, laughing when she should, nodding when she must, but a growing unease gnawed at the back of her mind.

Not fear. Not yet. Just… wrongness. Like something was bending the edges of the night in ways she couldn't see. She chalked it up to nerves. To the end of an era. To the knowledge that everything was about to change, and there was nothing she could do to stop it.

Still.

When she saw Lily again, standing alone at the tree-line, arms wrapped tight around herself, Emma felt her heart clench.

She took a step toward her twin, but a shadow moved through the trees behind Lily.

Quick. Silent. Gone before Emma could even focus. Her breath caught.

"Lil—" she started, but Lily turned, smiling, and gave a little wave.

Nothing behind her but rustling leaves. Emma shook herself. Paranoia. That's all. Still, she made a mental note to stick closer to Lily for the rest of the night. Just in case.

By the time the last speakers crackled and died and the final stragglers began stumbling up the track toward their cars, the quarry was littered with the detritus of celebration, empty bottles, trampled paper plates, broken necklaces, lost trainers. Emma stood at the edge of it all, feeling something inside her begin to unravel. The night had been fun. Hadn't it? And yet, that unease still clung to her, sticky as sweat.

Ben jogged up, breathless. "You ready?" he asked.

She spotted Tom, Maya and Lily climbing into Tom's battered Astra, already arguing about music. A few others were gathering by the road, laughing too loudly.

"Go on," she told Ben, forcing a smile. "I'll catch up."

"You sure?"

"Yeah. Just left something."

Ben hesitated, then nodded and jogged off. Emma started back toward the tree line where her sister last stood. The night was thick now. The quarry emptying fast. Every shadow felt too deep. The woods whispered and shifted. Emma stood very still. For a moment, just a heartbeat, she thought she saw something deeper in the trees. A flicker of movement. A pale face. But when she blinked, it was gone.

5

DI Tee / DC Zak

The morning started with another phone call.

Tee didn't even have her first sip of coffee when the buzz of her mobile cut through the hush of the office. She sat at her desk in the incident room, dark circles under her eyes and her blonde hair tied back in a sleek, low bun. The sky outside was a sheet of dull grey, a warning of storms to come, and she had that gnawing feeling again. The one she trusted more than most reports. Something was wrong.

"Another one," Zak said, his voice tight as he came through the door, holding a tablet in one hand and his coffee in the other. "Council cleaners found it behind the Co-op bins this morning. Same as Cedar Lane."

Tee pushed her mug aside. "Number four?"

"Five," Zak corrected. "Someone called in another yesterday, but it got logged wrong. I pulled it from the community reports this morning." He handed her the tablet. The image on the screen was grainy and taken from a phone, but it showed enough.

A tabby cat, splayed open, its paws arranged precisely, the eyes missing. The body had been placed with symmetry, not dumped, not hidden. Displayed.

"Jesus," Tee muttered. "It's escalating."

Zak nodded grimly and dropped into the chair beside her, rubbing at his eyes. "You were right. This isn't someone being reckless. It's ritual. Planned. And it's getting bolder."

Tee scanned the photo again. The paws were crossed delicately. As if someone cared how it looked. Not just what it meant.

"They want us to see it," she said. "They're showing off."

She stood abruptly. Her chair rolled back and hit the desk behind her. "Let's go. I want to see it for myself. We're missing something."

*

They drove in silence most of the way, both thinking the same thing but not wanting to say it yet.

Zak finally broke it. "You think it's building to something else?"

Tee didn't answer right away. The wipers dragged across the windscreen, smearing the drizzle into lines. The roads were wet and the town looked washed out, blurred at the edges.

"I think whoever's doing this doesn't see animals as enough anymore," she said finally. "I think we're on a timer."

The Co-op car park was mostly empty when they pulled in. A lone cleaner stood by the back alley, hands shoved into the pockets of his hi-vis jacket, shifting nervously on his feet.

"This way," he said, without prompting, and led them behind the bins.

The stench hit first. Decay and copper. The body lay beneath a stack of discarded cardboard, precisely positioned in the centre of a painted yellow line, as if whoever had left it was marking a boundary.

Tee crouched down and studied the scene. She didn't touch anything, not yet. Forensics would want it clean. But she could see the pattern.

"Same as before," Zak said, softly. "Eyes missing, paws crossed. No blood on the surrounding ground. Which means it wasn't killed here."

"Taken elsewhere, then transported. Still no signs of panic. No mess," Tee added. "They're experienced. Or methodical."

She rose slowly and turned to Zak. "Tell me about the previous scenes. Let's line them up again."

Zak flipped open his notebook. "Cedar Lane. Tabby, mutilated but not displayed as precisely. Alley behind the old bookshop on Turner Street, ginger, similar positioning to this one. Third was on Marlow Park footpath, partially buried but still posed. Fourth, yesterday's call-in, found in a front garden, staged but sloppy. And now this one."

Tee chewed her lip. "They're getting neater."

"Or more confident."

She nodded once. "Which means the cooling-off period is shortening."

"Three days between the first two. Two days between the next. Then one."

They both paused.

"Tomorrow," Tee said.

Zak looked at her. "You think they'll strike again tomorrow?"

"No," she said, a dark edge creeping into her voice. "I think if it's a person they want, tomorrow's the day they take them."

Zak's face paled. "You're jumping ahead—"

"No," she cut him off. "I'm not. You know how these things go. They start small. Animals. Then they test control. Positioning. Dehumanising. And when that no longer satisfies"

"They escalate," Zak finished.

They stood in the rain for a moment longer, the drizzle soaking through their coats. A quiet hung between them, dense with knowing.

*

Back at the station, Tee called for a task force meeting.

Whiteboards were dragged into the incident room. Photos pinned up. Timelines drawn. A pattern began to emerge. The killings weren't random. They traced a path, a map through the town's quieter corners, like the killer was mapping out a circuit.

"What are they looking for?" Zak murmured as he stared at the lines connecting pins. "A route? A ritual?"

Tee stepped back and looked at the map. "Or victims."

She grabbed a marker and circled five key areas.

"Each location is within walking distance of a secondary school or sixth form centre. Three are on the route home for students. All late afternoon."

Zak blinked. "Jesus. You think they're watching the kids?"

Tee nodded. "I think they've been watching for weeks."

The silence that followed was thick and grim.

"Get the schools briefed," Tee barked, suddenly shifting into high gear. "All of them. Heads, pastoral staff, everyone. I want someone watching exits. CCTV checked. Foot patrols increased. We tell them we're watching for someone targeting pets. We don't tell them more than that yet."

Zak raised a brow. "You think they'll listen?"

"They'll listen when they see the photos."

*

It was nearly 9 p.m. when Tee sat alone in her office, eyes fixed on the whiteboard.

The fluorescent lights buzzed overhead, and outside, the rain finally gave way to clear skies. But the air felt thick still, like the storm hadn't really passed.

Zak poked his head in. "I brought you the thing you pretend you don't like," he said, holding up a chocolate bar.

Tee smiled faintly and took it. "Appreciate it."

He lingered in the doorway. "You okay?"

Tee glanced at the board. "I've done this too long, Zak. You start to feel the shifts in the air before they happen. And right now, it's all shifting."

He didn't say anything. Just stepped in and dropped into the chair across from her.

"I know what you're thinking," he said after a while. "That if we don't get ahead of this, we'll be chasing a killer instead of preventing one."

She looked at him, eyes sharp. "We're already chasing one."

Another silence.

Then Tee said, "Let's start checking the animal shelter records. Vet logs. Any young adults or teens who've shown signs of cruelty to animals in the last few years. Anyone with access. Work experience. Abandoned pets. We'll need a list of names. Teachers who flagged behaviour. People who slipped through the cracks."

"I think it's someone close enough to be invisible," she said. "Young enough not to raise suspicion. But smart. And quiet."

She leaned back in her chair and stared at the board again. "We need to think like them. What would be the next step?"

Zak followed her gaze. "They've shown power over something small. To them, it was practice. So next..."

"Something harder to catch," Tee said. "Something human."

They stared at the circled locations in silence, their shared dread deepening.

6

The first human will fall, all of the practice is finally going to come into play.

She doesn't matter. Not really. What matters is that it's the beginning. The first step in the game. A signal, a crack in the surface of their perfect little world.

Her name is Sarah Morgan. Seventeen. Attends a nearby sixth form college. She isn't part of them, not one of the golden five. But she floats near the edges, like a moth drawn to their warmth, their brightness. They don't notice her. That makes her perfect. Tortured sad soul, I'm ready to set her free.

Invisible. Unimportant. Disposable.

But now, she will be remembered. She will be heard.

I've watched her for weeks. Quiet. Always on her phone but never calling anyone. Walks home alone. Lives with a father who works nights and drinks during the day. A brother away at uni. No one would notice if she vanished for a while. Maybe not even right away.

She's the first piece in the puzzle I'm laying out. The first cut in the tapestry of their denial. The first tremor beneath their feet. The first

And they'll never see it coming.

*

It starts on a Wednesday. Rainy. Cold for July. I like it that way, the clouds sit heavy in the sky, low and grey like bruises. The sort of weather that settles into people's bones and makes them more pliable. More afraid.

Sarah leaves the library at around 5. I'm already there, waiting, nothing about me out of place. A hoodie. A backpack. Nobody pays attention. Nobody ever does.

She walks the same path home every day. Through the narrow cut between the old garages on Beechwood Lane. I'm there before her, just to the left of the last garage, behind the corrugated wall. I can smell the metal in the air. I can hear the soft thuds of her steps.

Five. Four. Three.

I step out.

She startles, but only a little. She doesn't run. Not yet.

"Sorry," I say, holding my palms up. "Didn't mean to scare you."

She offers a half-smile. Nervous. But polite. That's Sarah.

"That's okay," she says, brushing damp strands of hair from her face.

She starts to walk past.
That's when I reach out. Grip her wrist.

She freezes. Blinks. Confused, not yet afraid.

Then I tighten my grip.

"What—?"

I cover her mouth before she screams. The knife is small, thin. Surgical. She sees it. Her eyes widen.

I don't enjoy this part. People assume that killers must relish the kill, the scream, the blood, the gasp of realisation. I don't. That part's just necessity. A step. A task.
It's what comes after that matters.
I make it quick. Efficient. I know where to cut. The jugular, the angle of the blade, it's practiced now.

She slumps. Not like in films. It's slow, like she's melting into the ground. The warmth of her leaving her limbs.

And then it's quiet again.

Not too bloody. No mess. I know how to create a clean cut where the blood trickles rather than spurts. I'm meticulous.

Sarah disappears into the shadows of a world that doesn't see girls like her. And I begin the work.

*

The next part is the message.

I take her phone, her school ID, the little silver bracelet she wears on her left wrist. I clean the body. Pose her, not obscenely, but deliberately, laid out under the bridge near the old railway tracks. Somewhere they'll find her eventually.

There's no real sign of a struggle. But there will be signs if they know what to look for.

A mark in the mud from her shoe. The bracelet, left in her palm. Her phone, screen cracked, shoved between the slats of the wooden fence nearby. A single white flower tucked behind her ear.

A puzzle.

A beginning.

By the time they find her, two days have passed.

The group doesn't even notice. Why would they? So irrelevant to their lives.

They're busy posting filtered photos of smoothies and sunflowers, talking about uni offers and holiday plans. Laughing in cafes and on swings in the park, while just a few streets away, a girl lies still in the dark.

And I watch them.

Emma, so bright. So full of ease and charm. Always laughing the loudest, always in the centre. Not like her twin, sweet, strange Lily, always watching but never quite seen. Tom with his lopsided grin and subtle cruelty. Maya, with her fierce eyes and possessiveness. Ben, awkward and silent, always watching Emma, always a second too late to speak.

They're perfect.

They're everything.

And they have no idea what's coming.

*

The police arrive eventually. I watch from a distance. I've seen them before. They'll be trouble. They're good.

But they're too late.

Sarah is already gone. And the real game has already begun.
I hear the murmurs on the street.

"Things like this don't happen here."

"She was so quiet."
"Never caused any trouble."

It's always the same script. Like people need to convince themselves they could've known her better. That they might've done something if they had just looked closer.

But they didn't. They never do.

And they won't see me either.

*

That night, I sit in the room, the walls covered with newspaper clippings, maps, photographs. Strings of red and black thread run between them, not because I need them, that's just the kind of cliché people expect, but because it amuses me.

At the centre, a photo.

The golden 5. Wishing to have the summer of their lives.

Pinned together like butterflies in a box.

Sarah was the first.

The message.

The question.
Next comes the answer.

*

I go back to Cedar Lane that evening. Back to where the first body, the cat was found. There's tape up now. A soft memory of caution.

I leave something new there.

Not a body.

A clue.

Sarah's student card. Washed clean. Laminated in plastic. Hung from a nail driven into the trunk of the tree nearest the alleyway.

It swings in the wind, quiet and purposeful.

By the time they find it, I'll be gone again.

*

The city breathes around me. Shops closing. Music thumping through car doors. People laughing into their phones, kissing on benches, screaming at children, walking dogs. And I walk through it all unseen. Because I don't wear a mask. I don't need one.

I smile. I nod. I hold doors open. I make small talk with the cashier. I help the old woman carry her bags. I am whoever they want me to be.

And none of them will see it coming.

*

Sarah is the hot topic now. Her photo in the newspaper is school-issued, poorly lit, unsmiling. They always choose the worst photos.

The headline says: "Tragedy as Teen Found Dead - Police Appeal for Witnesses."

Tragedy.

What a strange word for inevitability.

*

I watch as the golden 5 slowly begins to feel it.

They brush it off, just like they always brush anything serious off. The world bends to them. They don't believe in the possibility of someone like me.

The game has begun.

This is only the start.

They won't understand yet.

But soon, they will.

Soon, they'll regret everything.

Part Two

7

Emma

It started as a rumour. A whisper on social media, so quiet at first that I almost scrolled past it. One of those posts with grainy pictures and too many hashtags. A girl missing. A sixth form student. Another one of us.

Her name was Sarah Morgan.

The post came from someone at Willow College, one of the neighbouring sixth forms. I'd seen Sarah around at a few local events, school fairs, community fundraisers, the odd birthday party where our social circles lightly overlapped. She was the kind of girl who moved at the edges of things: quiet, observant, always tucked into the corners with a paperback in her hands or a cup of lemonade clasped neatly between her fingers. There was a stillness to her, like she didn't need to perform the way so many others did. Bookish, yes, but not in a cliché way, more like someone whose mind was always elsewhere, tuned to a frequency the rest of us hadn't quite figured out yet.

She was usually surrounded by a small, tight-knit group of equally understated girls, the ones who didn't chase attention but had a quiet, unshakable bond that made them seem untouchable in their own way. They'd sit cross-legged on the grass while the rest of us danced or shouted over music, heads tilted toward each other, laughing at things no one else heard. Like us, they weren't the kind of people who made waves or broke rules. Not popular, not outsiders either, just well-liked. Known. Safe.

Sarah had that sort of face people felt comfortable around: soft features, thoughtful eyes, a smile that never quite stretched too wide. Teachers liked her. Parents praised her. You'd trust her to look after your cat or tutor your little sister. She didn't stir drama. She didn't raise her voice. She didn't draw attention.

Not someone you'd expect to disappear.

And yet, she had. As if she'd been plucked out of this carefully woven community without so much as a ripple. And that, more than anything was what made it so unsettling. At first, I didn't think much of it. People exaggerate. Teenagers vanish for a night and come back when they've cooled off. I figured it was that kind of thing. One of those stories that burns through the feed and fizzles out once everything's fine. But by the time I woke up the next morning, it was clear: Sarah hadn't come home. She hadn't been at a friend's house. She hadn't replied to any messages. She was just... gone.

My phone buzzed constantly, messages from Maya, from Ben, even from Tom. A shared unease threaded through every word, every emoji that couldn't quite mask the tension.

"This is getting weird, right? All those cats now this"
"Em, you said you had a weird feeling"
"Everyone said that this isn't like her."

They were all saying the same thing, even if none of us wanted to admit it.

I lay on my bed, blinds half-drawn against the heavy morning sun, phone in my hand, watching Sarah's photo get shared over and over. In it, she was smiling softly, eyes tilted downward like she wasn't quite comfortable with the camera. It didn't feel like a missing poster. It felt like a memorial.

Lily knocked lightly on my door mid-morning. She didn't say anything, just looked at me with that quietly sad expression she wore more often lately, her arms folded across her chest, her eyes soft.

"I saw the news," she said.

I nodded. "It's awful."

She hesitated, then asked, "You going to the quarry tonight?"

"Yeah. Everyone wants to meet up."

She didn't reply straight away. Just lingered in the doorway like she had something else to say. Then she gave a small shrug.

"Don't go, this feeling is getting worse… I'm so scared" she said as tears streamed down her face.

I rushed over to her, 'Lil, oh Lily, it's okay, you're okay, this is all just a freak coincidence.' Lily nodded and attempted to dry her eyes.

"Okay." She said, but I know she didn't believe me.

Lily had been quieter than usual since school ended, she really internalises every situation. She's struggles with anxiety and depression, this is why I desperately need to protect her. On top of all of this chaos, it was the change, the shift from the routine we'd all known since we were kids. It was hitting her harder than the rest of us. And I got it. Uni was coming, and nothing was going to be the same. Everything was in that strange in-between place. Familiar, but already slipping.

That night, the quarry was quiet when we arrived.

No music. No shouting. Just the crackle of a fire and the occasional rustle of trees as a warm breeze moved through. Summer had softened into something strange and uncertain.

Maya was already there, sat close beside Tom. She barely looked up when I joined them. Ben came a few minutes later, carrying snacks he pretended not to have brought just to impress us.

Everyone was trying to act normal. But we weren't.

There was an unspoken weight between us. It sat behind every joke, every sidelong glance.

"She could've just run away," Tom said at one point, breaking a long silence. "It happens."

"No, it doesn't," Maya said sharply.

Tom frowned. "You don't know that."

Maya didn't reply. She stared at the fire, her jaw clenched.

I picked at the label on my drink bottle, not looking at anyone. I didn't want to take sides. Didn't want to argue. Not tonight.

Ben shifted closer to me, speaking quietly. "Do you think something… happened to her?"

The question hung between us, heavy and awful.

I didn't want to answer. But he was asking what we were all thinking.

"I don't know," I said. "I hope not."

Another long silence.

The fire popped suddenly, making Maya flinch.

"God," she muttered. "This is stupid. Why are we even out here?"

"To feel normal, to have the best summer before we all move away?" I offered, though I didn't believe it. Nothing felt normal anymore.

We stayed a while longer, talking in slow circles, words losing meaning.

No one mentioned Lily. No one asked why she wasn't there. She was always quiet. Always drifting on the edge of things. People didn't notice when quiet people stopped showing up. Maybe this is what happened to Sarah, she slipped through the cracks.

I thought of her sitting at home alone, drawing, maybe. Or curled in her bed with a book she wouldn't finish. The house had felt hollow when I left. Lily was right, I shouldn't have come, this isn't right.

Eventually, we drifted home. One by one. Like leaves breaking from a branch.

*

The next morning, Sarah's face was on the local news. The school released a statement. Her parents did too, a tearful clip of them standing beside a police officer, asking anyone with information to come forward.

It didn't feel real.

I watched the footage in the kitchen while eating cereal I couldn't taste. Mum said something about it being awful, shaking her head. Lily sat beside me, her hands wrapped around a cup of tea. She was still in her pyjamas. Still quiet. We didn't talk about it. We didn't need to.

*

Over the next few days, the town changed. It was subtle at first, more patrol cars on the main roads, more suspicious glances between neighbours. But soon, the fear settled in. Like smog. People stopped letting their kids walk home alone. Dog walkers kept to daylight. School group chats filled with speculation and warnings. There were rumours. So many rumours.

Someone said Sarah had been seen at the train station. Someone else claimed she'd run off with a boy from another town. Another person, who no one could name directly, said her sketchpad had been found by the canal, pages torn out. None of it felt real. And none of it brought us closer to the truth.

What stuck with me most was something Ben said during a call late one night.

"She wasn't the kind of girl people noticed," he said. "You know? She was… invisible. Until now."

And he was right. Just like Lily, that's what made it worse. Why did I have this feeling something bad was about to happen to Lily.

Sarah was the kind of girl no one would remember if she missed a party. The kind no one texted first. She was kind, sure. Smart. Quiet. But invisible. A background character in someone else's story.

And now, she was all anyone could talk about.

*

Lily didn't come to the quarry again. She didn't really go anywhere.

She spent most of her time in her room, drawing. I found some of her sketches left on the kitchen counter once, delicate pencil lines, scenes from memory. One of them was the quarry fire, drawn in fine detail, shadows stretching away from the flames like hands.

I asked if she was okay. She said yes, but her eyes looked far away. I knew she was lying, this whole situation was taking its toll on her.

*

That weekend, we met at the park.

Fewer of us this time. The others had started to drift away, finding excuses to stay home. The missing girl cast a long shadow, even over the brightest days.

Maya was tense, picking at her nails. Tom was quieter than usual, offering us all half-hearted jokes that didn't land. Ben sat beside me again, watching the trees more than the fire.

"She's still missing," he said. "It's been days."

"Police are still looking," I offered. "They'll find something."

"I don't think they will."
There was something about the way he said it. Final. Tired.

"Why not?"

Ben hesitated. "Because if they were going to find her, they would've already."

We were quiet for a long time after that. No one knew what to say anymore.

*

On the walk home, I stuck to the main road. It was late, and the town felt different at night now. The warm evenings had started to feel hostile, every shadow stretching longer than it should. A car passed. A curtain twitched in one of the houses. Somewhere in the distance, a dog barked.

I reached our front gate and hesitated, staring up at the dark windows.

The house looked normal. Still. But I couldn't shake the feeling that something, somewhere, was watching.

I crept upstairs and paused outside Lily's room, the door slightly ajar. The soft scratch of her pencil had stopped, she must've fallen asleep. I knocked gently, just in case, but there was no answer.

Pushing the door open a little more, I peeked in. Lily was curled up beneath her blanket, her breathing steady, one arm tucked under her pillow. Her desk lamp was still on, casting a warm pool of light across her sketchpad and scattered pencils.

I stepped in and quietly turned the lamp off, glancing at the open page on her desk. It was another one of her dreamy, abstract pieces, dark swirls of trees and night sky blending together. Beautiful. Melancholic. Typical Lily.

She always said drawing helped when things felt heavy. And lately, things had been very heavy.

I gently pulled the blanket higher over her shoulder and backed out, closing the door softly behind me.

*

By Monday, the posters were everywhere.

They appeared overnight, pinned to notice boards, taped to shop windows, posted at bus stops and the community hall. Sarah's face stared out from every corner of town. Each poster a silent plea.

Have you seen me?

There were candlelit vigils held in the school courtyard and outside the community centre, flickering flames casting long, trembling shadows across tear-streaked cheeks and clasped hands. People came wrapped in scarves and grief, holding photographs of Sarah, the same image printed over and over: her school portrait, smiling shyly in a navy jumper. Her name was whispered like a prayer. Songs were sung, soft and wavering, and someone always broke down before the second verse.

Volunteers turned out in droves, their high-vis jackets dotting the edges of the woods like fireflies. They trudged through brambles and mud, calling her name into the silence, clinging to hope long after common sense had started to fray. Some brought dogs, others maps, some just brought a sense of purpose. Drones whirred overhead, scanning the cold, dark surfaces of the nearby lakes, as if technology might find what the human eye had missed. The local news set up near the footpath, their vans casting long cables across the grass like veins, pumping footage out to the nation.

At Sarah's school, uniformed officers stood posted at the gates, their expressions unreadable, a visible reminder that this wasn't a story, it was real, and it was close. They watched the students like sentinels, while behind them, the school building loomed quiet, tense. The flag flew at half-mast.

We watched it all unfold from behind screens. Grainy phone footage reposted a hundred times. Livestreams. Blinking group chats. News alerts. We consumed it from the safety of our living rooms, fingers curled around mugs of tea we'd forgotten to drink. We refreshed threads, speculated in whispers, sent heart emojis when someone shared a post about staying hopeful. We were part of it, and also miles away. At a distance that felt comfortable. Manageable.

Until it didn't.

"We should do something," Maya said one afternoon, pacing my room.

"Like what?" I asked.

"Help search. Put up posters. I don't know — *something*."

Tom sat on my desk chair, spinning lazily. "It's not like we knew her."

Maya stopped pacing. "She was one of us. Don't you get that? That could've been *anyone*."

Tom looked uncomfortable. For once, he didn't argue.

Ben had gone quiet again. He sat beside me on the bed, staring at the carpet.

"I think she's gone," he whispered, barely audible.

Maya shot him a look. "Don't say that."

"I don't mean it like, I just mean, she's not... She's not coming back like before. If she does, she won't be the same."

The room fell silent again.

I hated how right he sounded.

*

Later that week, Lily came downstairs mid-morning, still in her pyjamas tucked under an oversized hoodie, headphones hanging loose around her neck, and smudges of charcoal dusting her fingertips like bruises she hadn't noticed. Her sketchbook was clutched to her chest, pages fanned and curling from use.

"Going for a walk," she said simply, her voice flat, almost distracted as if her mind was already three streets away.

Mum looked up from behind her laptop at the kitchen table, a pair of glasses slipping slightly down her nose. "Where?" she asked, the question automatic but edged with concern she tried to mask.

"I need more charcoal," Lily said. "And pencils. I'm running low."

There was a pause, just long enough to notice the faint tremble in her sleeve as she reached for her phone.

I stood by the sink, drying a mug, watching her in that way you do when something feels slightly... off, even if you can't name it. Her eyes didn't quite meet ours. Her hair was scraped back in a messy twist, and she hadn't bothered with shoes yet. She looked fragile in a way that made me ache, like glass someone had already cracked but hadn't shattered.

"I'll just go to that shop on Brantree Road," she added, already moving toward the door, slipping her feet into her trainers without untying the laces. "Won't be long."

I followed her with my eyes as she crossed the street carefully, like the road was unfamiliar. Her shoulders were hunched slightly against the late spring air, even though the sun was out and warm against the pavement. Her sketchbook was still under her arm, as if she might stop and draw something mid-journey. That was Lily always looking closer than the rest of us. Seeing what others missed.

I had the sudden urge to call out after her, to tell her to wait, that I'd come with her. To say something meaningless but reassuring, like "be careful" or "text me when you get there," even though the shop was only ten minutes away. But I didn't. I just stood there, one hand pressed against the cool kitchen counter, the other clutching a dish towel that I'd forgotten I was holding.

She disappeared around the corner, swallowed by the curve of the street, and the house felt quieter without her.

I told myself it was fine. That she did this all the time. That walks helped her think, clear her head, find rhythm again when the world got too loud.

But still, I found myself glancing at the clock. Watching the second hand tick with unnecessary focus. Waiting for the sound of the gate creaking open, for the key in the door.

The silence stretched too long.
And the unease never left.

*

Two more days passed.

Still no sign of Sarah.

Her face stared out from every lamppost and community board eyes wide, caught in the stillness of a moment long gone. A school photo, probably the most recent anyone had, printed onto cheap paper that fluttered in the breeze. Rain had smudged some of the ink. A few flyers were already curling at the edges, edges browned from sun and time, as if even they were beginning to give up.

The whole town was starting to unravel. You could feel it in the air, something taut and fraying, like a thread pulled too tight. The usual rhythms of daily life had shifted. People who once exchanged easy greetings now barely nodded. Neighbours kept their curtains drawn well into the morning, and doors were double-locked even in daylight.

There was a silence beneath everything. Not peaceful, anxious. Suspicious.

Trust, once easy and unconscious, had evaporated. Friendships strained under quiet doubts. Families whispered more than they spoke. On the streets, eyes lingered just a second too long. Innocent questions sounded like accusations. Conversations cut short when others drew near.

Even the shops felt colder. The supermarket aisles were filled with people who moved slower, their baskets half-full. At the café, the usual hum of chatter had turned into a low murmur, as if people were afraid to speak too loudly, in case it made things worse.

The days were warm, but the sun felt dimmer somehow, like it was shining on the wrong town. Even the wind had a strange edge to it, brushing against skin with a kind of urgency that made you glance over your shoulder.

And the birds they still came, but they weren't singing. They perched on fences and rooftops, restless, tilting their heads like they were listening for something too. Like they could sense it, the unease, the waiting, the slow darkening that no one wanted to name.

And under it all, the question hung, heavy and silent: Where was Sarah?

*

We went to the quarry again.

Just me, Ben, and Maya this time.

Tom had messaged earlier, something vague about helping his parents clear out the garage or fix a fence — I couldn't remember. The excuse felt thin, and the silence after it even thinner. He just didn't want to come. I didn't blame him.

The quarry had changed.

It was still the same place on the outside, the deep bowl of rock surrounded by trees, the wide open sky above like a yawning mouth, but it no longer felt like the secret haven we'd once claimed as ours. The wind moved differently now. The stillness felt heavier.

The fire burned low in the centre, crackling softly, barely enough to warm our hands. Its light flickered against the jagged stones, making shadows twitch along the cliff walls like they were alive.

Ben sat close to the flames, arms looped around his knees, his expression distant, eyes fixed on nothing. He hadn't said much since we got there, and even now his voice came out quiet, like he was afraid the quarry might listen.

"She's still missing," he said. "No one's heard a thing."

His words felt like they'd been pulled straight from the headlines, and yet they hung heavier in the air out here, like they didn't belong to a newspaper, but to us.

Maya didn't answer.

She stood off to the side, half in shadow, her arms crossed tightly across her chest. Her hair moved slightly in the breeze, but the rest of her was still. Watchful. Her face was unreadable, but her silence said enough.

I tilted my head back and looked at the stars, pinpricks of light scattered across the sky, indifferent and unreachable. I tried to remember how they used to look. How we used to lie on the quarry floor, laughing at shapes we saw in the constellations, inventing stories about comets and space explorers and impossible futures.

Now all I could see were points of light above a place that didn't feel safe anymore. A place that felt like it was waiting for something terrible to happen.

"There's a darkness in this place," Maya said suddenly.

Her voice cut through the silence, sharp and strange.

Ben turned to look at her. "What do you mean?"

She didn't answer right away. She stared into the shadows at the edge of the quarry like she was trying to see something hidden.

"I don't know," she said finally. "It's like… it gets into people. Twists them. When we're out here, we're not really ourselves. Have you noticed that?"

I swallowed, throat dry.

She wasn't wrong. I had felt it too, something just under the surface. A restlessness. A cold that didn't come from the wind. Like the quarry was more than a place. Like it was watching us back.

No one spoke for a while. The fire crackled. A branch snapped in the woods behind us and we all flinched, just slightly.

I looked at Maya, still standing stiffly on the edge of the firelight. Her jaw tight. Her eyes reflecting flames.

I wanted to say she was overreacting. That we were all just shaken and tired and trying to make sense of something that didn't have a shape yet. But the words didn't come.

Because I'd been feeling it too.

And maybe the scariest part was that I couldn't tell if it was coming from the quarry… or from us.

*

When I got home that night, the house was quiet, too quiet. No hum of the TV, no low chatter from Mum's office upstairs. Just the soft clink of a spoon against a pot and the low hiss of something simmering on the stove.

Lily was in the kitchen, her back to me, haloed in the warm amber glow of the under-cabinet lights. She was barefoot, her hoodie sleeves pushed up, and there were faint smudges of charcoal on her wrist, like she'd wiped her hands and forgotten about it.

She turned as I stepped in, offering me a small smile, gentle and worn at the edges.

"Hey," she said quietly. Her voice was soft, like she didn't want to break the stillness that had settled in the house. "You okay?"

I nodded, dropping my bag by the door. "Yeah. Just tired."

She studied me for a second, as if checking for cracks, then turned back to the pot. "It's tomato," she said. "There's not much else left."

She handed me a bowl, her fingers brushing mine, warm from the steam. We sat at the kitchen island, across from each other, the only sound the occasional clink of our spoons and the low hum of the fridge.

The soup was hot, comforting in the way that only something simple could be. But the quiet between us wasn't comfort, it was waiting.

After a few minutes, Lily broke it.

"I was down by the lake earlier," she said, not looking up. "Sketching. It was peaceful."

I nodded, not sure what to say. I hadn't been to the lake since Sarah vanished. The idea of it silent and vast unsettled me.

Lily glanced up, her eyes shadowed. "You ever get the feeling that something's ending?"

The question hit harder than I expected. I paused, my spoon suspended halfway to my mouth.

"What do you mean?" I asked carefully.

She stirred her soup, slow, deliberate circles. "Just that... things won't go back. Not to how they were. Like something's shifted. And now we're just waiting for the rest of it to catch up."

She looked up at me then, and her eyes, those same green eyes that matched mine in every mirror, looked older somehow. Like she'd seen something she wasn't meant to.

I didn't know how to answer.

Because I'd been feeling it too.

That strange, breathless tension like the air before a storm.
The sense that the world was tipping just slightly off
balance. That something invisible had started moving in
the dark.

And once it started, it wouldn't stop.

*

The next day, the police presence in town doubled. They
cordoned off part of the woods near the water treatment
plant. News crews lined the streets, cameras pointed at
every move. Forensics vans came and went, flashing white
suits visible in the gaps between trees.

Someone said a piece of clothing had been found.
Someone else said it was her shoe. The rest was
speculation. But that was enough.

*

That night, the town didn't sleep. You could feel it a kind
of breathless unrest hanging in the air like smoke. Every
house on our street was lit up like Christmas, except there
was nothing to celebrate. Porch lights flickered. Upstairs
windows glowed. Curtains hung half-open as if people

couldn't decide whether they wanted to hide from the world or stare it down.

Inside those houses, families huddled close not saying much, just listening. Watching. Phones clutched tightly in hands, screens lighting up with every new notification, every unconfirmed rumour passed through group chats like wildfire.

Lily sat beside me on the sofa, her legs folded up under her, wrapped in one of Dad's old jumpers. She hadn't spoken in over an hour. Her fingers played absentmindedly with a loose thread on the cuff. The TV flickered in front of us, casting a blue pallor across her face. It made her look like a ghost.

The news anchors spoke in that strange, rehearsed calm voices carefully measured, almost too composed, like if they lost control for even a second, everything would fall apart.

The screen cut to a press conference outside the station. I recognised the detective from earlier sharp-eyed, unsmiling, the kind of woman who looked like she could tear a person apart just by staring at them long enough. Her voice rang out, clipped and forceful.

"We are treating this as a high-priority case. We are doing everything in our power to bring Sarah home safely."

The same line, repeated like a chant. I wondered if they believed it.

Lily didn't look away from the screen, but I could feel the tension in her body coiled tight like a wire. I wanted to say something, anything, but the words dried in my throat.

Outside, a dog barked once sharp and sudden then stopped. Somewhere down the street, a car door slammed. Every sound felt louder than it should've been.

Still no sign of Sarah. No messages. No sightings. Just that awful, echoing silence.
And something worse the creeping realisation settling in everyone's chest like cold lead:

Sarah hadn't just disappeared.

Someone had taken her.
Someone nearby.

Someone who knew how to stay quiet. How to blend in.

Someone who might've smiled at her once. Said hi at the shop. Lived a few doors down.

And they were still out there.

Watching. Waiting.

8

DI Tee / DC Zak

The body was too clean.

Detective Inspector Tee stood just outside the taped perimeter, arms folded tightly, her expression unreadable beneath the low brim of her cap. The early morning sun had only just begun to rise, and already it felt too bright, its light too sharp against the stark reality in front of her.

The girl lay nestled in a bed of flattened gorse and bracken at the bottom of a disused railway embankment. She was dressed in the same clothes she'd last been seen wearing, a pale hoodie, dark jeans, and white trainers, now smudged with soil. Her limbs were arranged deliberately, like a doll, single white flower tucked behind her ear. Arms folded gently over her chest. Hair brushed away from her face. There was no sign of violence. No visible blood. No torn clothing.
Just stillness.

Zak stood to her left, quietly flipping through his notebook. He looked pale, even under the morning light, curls damp from the drizzle that had passed earlier. He adjusted his glasses, squinting down at the scene.

"Dog walker found her," he said quietly. "Name's Walter Hughes. Lives three streets down. He walks this way every morning. Saw something white by the bushes. Thought it was litter until he got closer."

Tee's jaw tightened. "What time?"

"Five twenty-two. Called it in at five thirty. Paramedics arrived at five forty, confirmed no pulse. Scene was sealed by six."

She crouched down slightly, keeping her distance, eyes scanning every inch of the clearing. There was no struggle. No broken branches. No disturbed dirt. If Sarah Morgan had died here, she had done so peacefully. But Tee knew better.

"She was moved," Tee said quietly. "This isn't where she died."

Zak nodded, not looking up from his notes. "There's no drag marks. No smudged footprints leading in or out. Whoever brought her here was careful. Knew what they were doing."

Tee stood, brushing her palms on her trousers. "Or they've done it before."

Forensics worked quietly around them, gloved hands moving with practiced precision. The chirp of a camera shutter clicked somewhere behind her. A flash illuminated the girl's face briefly, too pale, too still.

"No sign of restraint," Zak murmured. "Clothes are intact. No indication of sexual assault. Nothing obvious at least."

Tee scanned the horizon, her mind ticking through possibilities. "She didn't fight. She didn't run."

"Drugged?" Zak offered.

Tee nodded. "Toxicology will tell us more. But it's clean. Controlled."

They both fell silent for a long moment. The birds above them chirped cheerily in contrast to the scene.

Zak finally spoke again. "It's the escalation, isn't it?"

Tee turned toward him. "From the cats, yeah. This isn't just someone experimenting anymore. This is someone declaring themselves."

Zak looked back at Sarah's body. "And what are they saying?"
"That they're ready."

*

Back at the station, the atmosphere had shifted.

The incident room had always carried a quiet buzz, but now it hummed with real urgency. Sarah's school photo had already been pinned to the board, her eyes staring out under the word FOUND in bold red letters.

Tee and Zak moved like clockwork, briefing the forensics team, submitting statements, pushing CCTV requisitions. Every moment mattered now.

"She went missing Wednesday evening," Tee said, pointing to the whiteboard. "No one heard from her after 5p.m. Friends assumed she'd gone home. Her parents assumed she was with friends. That window, between seven and ten, that's our target."

Zak added, "Last seen on a bus stop camera near Westgate Avenue. She was walking north. Alone. No one nearby on the first two clips."

"But she didn't vanish into thin air," Tee said. "Someone was watching. Someone waited until there was no one around."

There was a knock at the door. PC Davies appeared, holding a tablet.

"Ma'am. You'll want to see this. Came in from a resident on Ashdown Crescent. Ring camera picked it up last night."

They gathered around as the footage played.

Sarah appeared on screen first, walking quickly, head down, arms wrapped around herself. She didn't look frightened. Just tired. Unaware.

Then, ten seconds later, a shadow.

It moved just at the edge of the frame. Barely a blur. A hooded figure, keeping distance but matching pace. Never too close. Never too far. Perfectly calculated.

Zak frowned. "We've got a timestamp?"

"5:35 p.m.," Davies replied. "Roughly thirty-five minutes after she left her study group."

Tee leaned in. "That figure doesn't hesitate. They know exactly where she's going."

Zak said, "And they're calm. No rush. No panic. They've done this before."

Tee's mind raced. "It's not a thrill kill. Not spontaneous. This is premeditated. Every detail."

She turned to Davies. "Pull every camera within a two-mile radius. I want vehicle footage, shop fronts, dash cams. If this person went anywhere, I want to know."

"And get digital forensics to go over Sarah's phone," Zak added. "Even deleted messages. Especially deleted messages."

Davies nodded and left.

Zak turned to Tee. "Do you think she knew them?"

Tee exhaled. "No signs of a struggle. No attempt to run. Either she was unconscious… or she trusted them."

They locked eyes. Both knew which possibility was worse.

*

It was late afternoon by the time Tee stepped outside, needing air. The sun was blazing now, almost cruel in its brightness. She leaned against the handrail near the back lot, rubbing her temples. Zak joined her after a moment, holding two coffees.

"I figured you hadn't eaten," he said, handing her one.
She took it gratefully. "Thanks."

They sipped in silence for a while, the distant sound of traffic the only background noise.

"I keep thinking," Zak said finally, "about that cat scene in the alleyway. Remember what you said? That it felt staged. Purposeful."

Tee nodded.

"This is the same," he continued. "The symmetry. The placement. It's not just murder. It's art."
Tee gave a bitter smile. "We've got a psychopath with an eye for aesthetics. Great."

*

That night, back in her flat, Tee sat on her sofa, laptop open, Sarah's photo displayed beside a map of her last known locations. Her face, bright hopeful, stared back at her, frozen in time. Seventeen years old. Barely a ripple when she vanished. It had taken eighteen hours before anyone reported her missing. Tee hated that. That she'd slipped through the cracks so easily.

She scrolled through the map, red dots marking Sarah's last movements. A second map lay beside it, the cat mutilation locations. Different streets, different days. But when she overlaid them, something shifted.

A ring.

She paused.

All the previous animal sites, they weren't random.
They'd created a boundary.

And Sarah had died inside it.

She sat back slowly, heart beating faster.

"Zak," she said aloud, reaching for her phone. "You need
to see this."

*

Meanwhile, Zak sat alone in his flat, half-finished case
notes open in front of him, untouched. His thoughts kept
drifting back to the footage. The way the shadow had
moved. Not rushed. Not erratic. Just… deliberate.

He opened a browser tab, typing quietly:
"Staged crime scenes. Serial escalation."

What came back wasn't comforting. Multiple cases. All
beginning with cruelty to animals. Graduating. Growing
bolder. More precise.

He leaned back in his chair. It wasn't about who the killer chose. It was about when they'd stop pretending they were playing. Because this wasn't a practice run anymore.

It had started.

And someone, someone right under their noses, was already planning the next move.

9

The first is always the hardest. They say that. And they're right. Not because of the act itself not for me. No. That part was... inevitable. Clean. Almost peaceful. What made it difficult was the silence afterward. The stillness. The waiting. The knowing.

Sarah didn't scream. Didn't beg. She barely spoke at all. And maybe that's what made her the right one. She'd been silent her whole life. She slipped through rooms like smoke, present but never noticed. So when she disappeared, it barely stirred the air.

Perfect.

She was my signal. The stone thrown into the water the ripples would come. Fear would bloom. The peace that this town wore like a mask would fracture, piece by piece.

And I would be watching.

I was careful that night. I always am. Gloves, plastic sleeves, burner phone off and buried in tin. I watched her walk home, footsteps light on the pavement. She didn't even see me. That was the thing about Sarah, always looking down, like the world might vanish if she dared lift her eyes.

She never saw me. Not until the very end. And even then, I think she knew.

Afterward, I stood just far enough from the crime scene to watch the chaos begin. The flashing blue lights. The hushed radio calls. The snapping of gloves. Officers moving like puppets across the cordon. The girl zipped up into a bag, so delicate, like they were afraid to break her a second time.

I felt nothing.
No regret. No triumph.
Only movement. Forward. Purpose.

I went home, took the long route through the fields, avoiding cameras I'd already mapped out months before. Every street, every blind spot, every house that had a doorbell cam, I knew them better than the people who lived there. I had to. They were sleepwalking. I was awake.

When I got back, I locked the door, pulled the blackout curtains tight, and turned on the desk lamp. Soft yellow light spilled across the desk, and there it was, waiting for me.

The notebook.

Not the kind you'd find in a school bag. Mine was leather-bound, the cover frayed at the edges. I ran a finger down the spine before flipping it open.

The list stared back at me, each name written in the same careful hand. Precise. Permanent.

Maya Brooks

Tom Grant

Ben Carter

Emma Shaw

And at the very top, scratched in darker ink, pressed so hard the paper had warped:

Lily Shaw

Lily.

She wasn't supposed to matter. Not to them. And yet, they made her the centre of everything, their jokes, their whispers, their silences. They laughed while she shattered. I watched her break. Slowly, over weeks. I watched her dim like a flame under glass, flickering, gasping for oxygen. No one reached in. No one cared.

But I did.

I saw her.

They say grief has stages. I didn't grieve. I didn't mourn. I changed. She gave me that. A different kind of awakening. The kind that sharpens your mind and hardens your heart. The kind that makes you see clearly.

They broke her. And now they would break, too.

But not like Sarah. No, Sarah's death was a message. The others needed something else. Something more intimate.

Fear.

I'd mapped them out. Where they lived. When they left the house. When they were alone. I didn't need to speak to them to know them. I knew everything already.

Maya, with her glittery lies and saccharine smiles. Always the loudest in the room. Always pretending she wasn't the one starting the rumours. She was high on the list after Sarah. Because she was the kind of person who needed to watch her world unravel before she realised it wasn't invincible.

I would show her.

Then Tom, popular, arrogant Tom. Captain of his own world, always with a cruel grin tucked behind his polished charm. He pushed things too far because no one ever told him no. He once cornered Lily outside the library, whispered things that left her shaking.

She never spoke about it. She didn't need to.

Ben came next. The quiet follower. The one who laughed too hard at jokes he didn't tell, who stayed silent when silence hurt more. Cowards like him were worse than the loud ones. They watched it happen. And they did nothing.

Then Emma.

I hesitated when I wrote her name.

Because Emma was different. She didn't always join in. But she didn't stop it either. She looked the other way. Even when Lily was right there, bleeding from a thousand invisible cuts.

Emma had the chance to change things. But she chose safety. She chose distance.

They all did.

Now, I was choosing justice.

Not courtroom justice, no, that's for the people who still believe in consequences. This wasn't about evidence or verdicts. This was about balance. What they took needed to be returned.

I flipped to the next page in the notebook. Beneath each name were columns: "Observation," "Schedule," "Weakness," "Next Move."

I'd been watching them for months.

I knew Maya always left her house at 7:48 a.m. exactly. She took the alley behind the shops because it was quicker, even though it was darker.

Tom jogged every evening at six. His AirPods in, music too loud to hear someone behind him.

Ben's mum worked nights. He was always home alone after nine. He never locked the back door properly.

Emma had a pattern too, always standing near the back wall at the quarry, always alone, always facing away from the woods.

They were so easy. So predictable.

And Lily… she watched them, too. I think that's why she pulled away near the end. She started seeing them for what they were. But by then, it was too late.

Now it's not.

Now I'm seeing for her. I will set her free.

I closed the notebook and slid it back into its hiding place, a hollowed-out panel beneath the floorboards. No one would find it. Not the police. No one.

They still don't see it. Even now, with Sarah dead and fear setting into their bones, they don't know what's coming. They're circling shadows, chasing the wrong scent.

I saw them today, the detectives.

Blondie and the handsome one with the glasses.

She's sharp. I'll give her that. She watches people like I do. She feels things that others ignore. But even she's behind. She thinks this is about escalation. Like I lost control.

She's wrong.

This isn't chaos.
It's art.
Each movement is deliberate. Each step choreographed. There's rhythm in this, structure. A narrative unfolding exactly how it's meant to.

They're only just reading chapter one.

I leaned back in my chair, listening to the house settle around me. The air was still, the clock ticking softly behind me. I liked that sound. It reminded me of inevitability.

Tick. Tock.

Their time is running out.

But not too fast.

I want them to feel it build. The cracks. The paranoia. The guilt. The questions that start to wake them up at night, did I say something? Did I do something? Could I be next?

Yes.

You could be.

You already are.

And when the next message is delivered, not a body, but something better, they'll start to understand.

Sarah was the stone. The others?

They're the flood.

10

Emma

The days after Sarah's death bled into each other like watercolour in the rain. Summer was supposed to feel bright, effortless. But now it hung over us like smoke, heavy, suffocating, lingering in the lungs.

Everyone grieved in different ways. Some talked too much, trying to fill the silence. Some drifted away. Others turned brittle, snappish, as if grief had sharpened them into something breakable. We were all pretending in different ways, but no one could pretend enough to make it feel normal.

We still met up, even though it felt wrong. The park, the café by the corner shop, the cliff edge at sunset, anywhere that held a fragment of who we used to be. But there was a tension there now, like we were sitting on a fault line, waiting for the ground to split.

Maya was the first to say it aloud.
"She didn't deserve it," she said one afternoon, her voice cracking as she stared into her half-melted milkshake. "She was just… quiet."

We all nodded. What else could we do? No one thought that something like this could happen in our sleepy market town. This town was safe, we had neighbourhood watch.

I'm starting to realise that maybe I had been sheltered my whole life, the world is dangerous.

Ben reached for her hand but didn't say anything. He hadn't said much since we'd found out. He just kept showing up, organising things, trying to force normality into the group like stuffing paper into a broken vase.

Tom paced. Always pacing. He'd grown twitchier, jumping at every noise, looking over his shoulder like he expected someone to be there.

And Lily… she was still Lily.

Quieter, maybe. But not strange. Just inward. Her silence was softer, gentler. She still came when I asked, still walked beside me on the way home. She just didn't speak much unless I asked a direct question. And even then, she answered with careful thought, like every word had weight.

I'd always known she kept a lot inside. She was like one of her drawings: intricate, detailed, but most people never looked close enough to see it. After Sarah's death, she started sketching more often. Not people, though, she said faces felt too close. Instead, she filled her notebook with houses half-buried in woods, overgrown paths, wildflowers creeping through fences.

"Do they mean something?" I asked once, peering over her shoulder.

She shook her head. "No. It just helps."

I worry about Lily, especially after that time, that horrible awful time she was in hospital. She's fragile and so sensitive, she tears up when she sees a killed badger at the side of the road. We were all carrying something. Some of us just carried it differently, Lily carries the weight of the world on her shoulders.

*

It had been two weeks since the news about Sarah shattered the town, and slowly, almost imperceptibly, things had begun to move forward not quite the same, but not entirely frozen anymore either.

The police were still investigating, of course. There were still missing posters curled at the edges on lampposts and taped to shop windows, now a little faded from rain and sunlight. People still lowered their voices when her name came up. But the urgency had dulled, numbed by the passing days and the inevitability of life continuing.

Sarah's funeral had been held three days earlier. A sea of black umbrellas. Tears on faces that looked stunned more than sad. A white coffin and flowers that didn't feel like enough. After that, something in the town began to shift.

Not heal, not yet but loosen. Like everyone had been holding their breath and could finally let out a slow, shaking exhale.

Summer began to find its rhythm again. The weather held steady in golden warmth. Kids returned to their bikes and ice cream vans began making their slow, familiar rounds. There were still whispers, still unease but also barbecues, music, laughter starting to float through open windows again.

And then came the leavers' BBQ.

One final time, we were all heading back to school. Not for lessons, not for stress, just to say goodbye properly to the classrooms, the lockers, the teachers who once terrified us and now just seemed human.

We arrived in waves, sunglasses on, bottles of lemonade in hand, like we were stepping out of a memory. It felt surreal walking those corridors again the walls covered in old posters and goodbye messages scrawled in Sharpie. Everything smelled faintly of cleaning spray and grass.

The sun was blazing down by the time we all gathered on the school field for the traditional students vs. teachers rounders game a silly, nostalgic ritual no one ever admitted to looking forward to but everyone loved. For a little while, we weren't grieving or speculating or second-guessing each other. We were just teenagers again, sweaty and laughing and shouting rules no one remembered.

Even Maya played. Maya, who avoided sweat the way most people avoided contagious disease, joined in full makeup, perfect lashes, fake nails and all. At one point, she hit a surprisingly decent ball and ran the bases squealing, holding her hair like it was her crown. It made everyone roar with laughter.

Tom was in his element, teasing the teachers with overly dramatic slides into base. Ben played too, running awkwardly but with surprising determination. Lily cheered from the sidelines, her sketchpad abandoned on the picnic blanket as she leaned into the moment. Even I felt lighter the kind of joy that sneaks up on you and wraps around your chest like sunshine.

Afterwards, we flopped on the grass, flushed and breathless, picking at burgers and passing crisps around. Someone had brought a speaker. There was music, half-dancing, plans for beach trips, for concerts, for late-night drives under the stars.

For the first time in what felt like months, the gang felt whole again. Solid. Balanced. Even Maya and Tom hadn't bickered once.

Lily looked more relaxed than I'd seen her in weeks a faint smile on her lips, a streak of charcoal smudged across one hand like a signature she'd forgotten to wipe off.

It was a good day. A needed day.

And then the first note showed up.

It was found near the lockers, folded neatly, no name, just one line written in tight, deliberate handwriting. The kind of line that sucked all the air from the corridor when someone read it aloud.

You don't know what you've done.

That was all. No context. No signature.

But something about it made everyone stop.

It was like a tiny crack had reappeared in the surface of our perfect day a warning, a whisper, a cold finger trailing down the spine.

The summer, it turned out, wasn't done with us yet.

*

It was folded tight and shoved through the slats of my locker door. For a second, I thought it was from Ben, he used to leave dumb drawings or messages for me when we were younger. But the paper was stiff, the handwriting sharp, almost angry.

The second note came two days later. Slipped into my bag. Lily had gone to get drinks. I was alone for maybe five minutes.

You'll pay for it soon.

That night, I sat on my bed and lined both notes side by side on my duvet. The handwriting was the same. The slant, the pressure of the pen. Neat but aggressive. Like someone writing too hard, like they were trying to force the ink to dig into the paper.

I felt cold all over.

Still, I said nothing. Not to Ben. Not to Maya. Not even to Lily.

It wasn't fear, exactly. It was something else. A kind of creeping dread I didn't want to name.

*

Things in the town grew quieter but not in any way that brought peace.

On the surface, everything looked calm. Police patrol cars still looped their usual routes, headlights sweeping across the streets like tired eyes. Shop windows were cluttered with safety notices, all bright fonts and exclamation marks, like warnings could fix what had already happened. Grief counsellors still handed out laminated leaflets outside cafés and community halls little folded promises of healing that most people accepted just to be polite and stuffed into coat pockets unread.

But underneath, the quiet had changed. It wasn't mourning anymore. It was suspicion.

The murmurs had started small in corners of pubs, between lowered voices at the post office counter. But now they were growing bolder, louder. People stopped whispering Sarah's name like it might summon bad luck, and started saying it with certainty, as if they knew things.

They didn't.

They talked about where she was found the edge of the woods, barely hidden. About the lack of struggle, the condition of her clothes, what the autopsy might have shown. The police had called it inconclusive. They said there were no signs of foul play. That they were still following every possible lead. But no one really believed them anymore.

Not really.

The official line that it was either a tragic accident or maybe even suicide didn't sit right with people. It was too neat. Too quiet.

So the town began to stitch its own version of the story.

Some blamed the pressure of exams. Others hinted at secrets, relationships, things Sarah had been keeping hidden. And then there were the ones who leaned in, just a little too eagerly, when the word murder was dropped. Their eyes lighting up with something sharp. Like it excited them.

Because a clean tragedy wasn't enough anymore. They wanted something darker. Something with teeth.

It was as if burying her had given everyone permission to start speculating out loud to treat her death like a puzzle, or a campfire story, or worse, entertainment.

And I hated them for it.

For the way they twisted her into something she wasn't. For how quickly grief curdled into gossip. For the way they all looked at each other a little differently now like anyone could be hiding something. Like danger could be living next door.

Because maybe it could.

And the worst part was, a small part of me was starting to wonder if they were right.

*

One evening, I walked home with Lily. The sun was low in the sky, stretched thin and bleeding orange across the rooftops, casting long, warped shadows over the pavement like the day itself was unraveling. The air was warm, but the breeze had a strange edge to it, like something unsaid moving between us.

Lily walked beside me, clutching her sketchbook tight against her chest, fingers smudged with graphite. Her headphones were looped around her neck, but they were silent. For once, she wasn't hiding behind music.

"I miss when everything felt simpler," I said, quietly the words slipping out before I could decide if I really meant them. "Like when we didn't have to think about all this. About Sarah. About… everything."

I wasn't expecting her to respond. I thought maybe she'd nod, or change the subject, like she usually did when things got too heavy.

But she didn't.

Instead, she glanced over at me, her eyes shadowed, her face calm in that unsettling way of hers. "Things were never simple," she said. "You just didn't see the cracks."

Her voice was steady, but it hit me like a slap.

I looked at her really looked. The girl I shared a face with, who could finish my sentences, who had been at my side for every version of our lives. But suddenly, she felt a little further away than before. Like she'd walked ahead of me, seen something I hadn't. Something I wasn't ready for.

Her words echoed in my head. You just didn't see the cracks.
It stuck with me because she was right. And I hated how right she was.

I'd always thought of myself as perceptive. Self-aware. The kind of person who could read a room, read a person, see through the bullshit. I'd even built my whole future on it, psychology, behaviour, patterns. But maybe I'd only ever been reading the surface. Skimming. Choosing to believe the good, the safe, the easy.

Had I been too naive? Too wrapped up in my own little world to notice that things had always been a little… off? That the people around me were more fractured than I allowed myself to see? That maybe Lily quiet, observant Lily had been carrying more than she ever said aloud?

The thought twisted in my stomach.

Maybe it wasn't that the world had changed since Sarah disappeared. Maybe it had always been this broken and I was only now waking up to it.

We kept walking, the sound of our footsteps filling the silence between us.

I didn't say anything else.

Because once you start seeing the cracks, it's impossible not to look for more.

*

Ben noticed first.
"You okay?" he asked during lunch at the cafe. "You seem... off."

I nodded too quickly. "Just tired."
"You'd tell me if something was wrong, right?"

"Of course."

It was a lie. But I needed to believe it. Needed someone to believe it.

*

One afternoon, as the heat clung to the pavement and the air felt thick with something unsaid, Maya pulled me aside just outside the café. Her manicured hand clamped around my wrist, too tight to be friendly.

"Has Lily said anything to you?" she asked, her tone flat, but her eyes scanning my face like I was a suspect.

I blinked. "About what?"

"She's just… off." Maya let out a short laugh, not kind. "I mean, I know she's always been a bit weird, floating around with that sketchbook like she's in some indie film no one asked for. But this is different. She's avoiding us."

I stiffened. "She's just quiet. She always has been."

Maya rolled her eyes. "Yeah, but at least she used to pretend to be part of things. Now it's like she's deliberately shutting us out. I asked if she wanted to come out tonight Tom, Ben, and me and she just stared at me. Didn't even blink. Rude, honestly."

"She's coping in her own way," I said, more defensive than I meant to be.

Maya snorted. "Coping? Please. Lily's always been fragile. You know that. She doesn't do well with pressure. Remember last year when she, you know, and now…

this?" She shook her head slowly. "I'm just saying, I wouldn't be surprised if she snapped."

Her voice lowered, more pointed now. "If she tells someone something she shouldn't that's not just her problem anymore."

I stared at her. "What are you even talking about?"

Maya smiled, but it didn't reach her eyes. "Come on, don't play dumb. Its not like we we nice to Sarah. People are talking. The last thing any of us need is Lily making it worse."

She stepped back, letting go of my arm, brushing invisible lint from her jacket like the conversation bored her. "Just... keep an eye on her. For everyone's sake."

I nodded, slowly, even though everything in me screamed not to.

Because deep down, I knew this wasn't about concern. It was about control.

And Maya? Maya didn't like it when things or people slipped out of hers.

*

At home, I opened my drawer and took out the notes again.

Four now.

You don't know what you've done.
You'll pay for it soon.
You let it happen.
She trusted you.

Each one was sharper than the last. Like whoever was sending them had gone from warning to blaming.

But for what?
What did they think I'd done, I didn't do anything.

*

I started locking my bedroom window. Checking behind me on the way home. Keeping my phone clutched tight even during short walks. Still, the feeling never left me, like something was following just out of sight.

Ben messaged me one night.

We should do something for Sarah. A memorial. I know the funerals done, but something planned by us and not the adults... you know?
It felt right. Something to take back a little control.

We met at the quarry, just a small group. Maya brought candles. Tom carved Sarah's name into a stone. I brought flowers.

As the sun dipped below the horizon, we lit candles and sat in silence.

"I feel like someone's watching us," Maya whispered.

Ben shifted beside her. "It's just the wind."

But I felt it too.

That weight.

That hush just before something breaks.

*

The tension was growing again. People whispered behind hands. Everyone was cautious. The police put out a press release to announce that Sarahs death was being treated as suspicious

Rumours started spinning.
That Sarah had been targeted.

That someone was next.

No one said it out loud, but the fear was spreading. I could feel it in the way people stared too long. In the way conversations stopped when I walked past.

I wasn't imagining it anymore.

*

I took a long walk after lunch, I needed to clear my head. I stuck to the main roads, but made sure to take my time. When I got home, I found Lily in the garden by the summer house, arms folded tight, sketchbook hugged to her chest. She looked pale.

"Hey," I said. "You okay?"

She nodded. "Just tired."

I hesitated. "You sure?"

She shook her head. "Nothing. Just… forget it."

I wanted to press her. Ask what she meant. But the fear in her eyes stopped me.

I didn't want her to close off more than she already had.

*

118

That night, I sat in bed with all of the notes laid out in front of me, a perfect, terrifying row of secrets. My duvet was pushed back, the room too hot, too still. The paper curled slightly at the corners from how many times I'd unfolded and refolded them, but the words those sharp, cold words stared back at me like they had teeth.

The handwriting wasn't dramatic. It wasn't angry. It was neat. Deliberate. Like whoever had written them hadn't needed to yell to be heard. That somehow made it worse.

I read them over and over again, as if repetition might unlock some kind of clarity, some buried memory that would explain everything. But it didn't. All it did was feed the gnawing sense that something was deeply, irreversibly wrong.

Someone out there knew something.

Someone believed *I* had done something terrible.

And I didn't know who.

But the worst part the part that made my skin crawl and my throat tighten wasn't the accusation. It wasn't the threat. It wasn't even the idea that someone was watching me.

It was the whisper in my own head that asked:

What if they're right?

Because the truth was, I didn't know what had happened to Sarah.

Not really.

I had no answers, only flashes her face at that last party, a strange look in her eyes, something she said that didn't make sense until now. I remembered moments. Gaps in conversation. People leaving and returning and no one really keeping track. I remembered that feeling in my stomach, something shifting beneath the surface, just out of reach.

What if I missed something?
What if I *did* something?
What if I had a piece of the truth and didn't even know it?
I rubbed my hands over my face and stared at the ceiling, willing myself to breathe. Outside, the street was quiet, almost eerily so, no cars, no voices, just the occasional creak of the house settling. I used to love the quiet. Now it felt like a trap.

A floorboard creaked downstairs. Probably the boiler, or Mum pacing in the kitchen again. But suddenly, I didn't feel safe in my own home. I didn't feel safe in my own head.

Because the line between guilt and innocence wasn't as clean as I used to think it was.

And the longer I stared at those notes, the more I felt like something inside me was coming undone like maybe, just maybe, I *had* done something.
Something I couldn't remember.

Something I didn't want to.

*

I didn't sleep. I couldn't.
The next morning, I made a decision.

I packed the notes into an envelope and slipped them into my school bag.

I needed to tell someone.

Not Maya.

Definitely not Tom.

Not Ben.
Not even Lily.

But maybe… the police.

Because something was happening to us.

Something dark.

And it wasn't going to stop on its own.

11

DI Tee and DC Zak

The briefing room was quiet, the usual hum of activity subdued. Tee spread out the maps on the table, pointing to the red dots.

"These are the locations of the mutilated cats. When overlaid, they form a boundary. Sarah's last known location is here, at the centre."

Zak leaned in, examining the pattern. "It's deliberate. Marking territory. Are we sure the cat killer and Sarahs murderer are connected?"

"Definitely. And the escalation from animals to humans fits the profile we've been reading about." Tee fired back.

Zak nodded, recalling the articles detailing the progression of violent offenders. The link between animal cruelty and human violence was well-documented, with many serial killers starting with animals before moving on to people.

"We need to revisit the earlier cases," Tee said. "There might be overlooked connections."

Re-examining the Cases

They spent the day poring over reports, photos, and witness statements. Each case of animal mutilation had been treated in isolation, dismissed as random acts of cruelty. But now, patterns emerged—similar methods, specific locations, and a timeline that suggested a calculated progression.

"Look at this," Zak pointed to a report. "This cat was found with its organs removed, and the body positioned deliberately. It's not just killing; it's staging."

Tee's eyes narrowed. "Perfecting the method."

They pinned up the evidence, gruesome photographs, timelines, witness statements, until the entire board became a map of escalation, a slow-burning fuse they were only now seeing had always led to Sarah.

The Psychological Profile

They consulted with a forensic psychologist, Dr. Elaine Harper, who specialised in criminal behaviour.

"Staging is about control," Dr. Harper explained. "The perpetrator wants to manipulate the narrative, to mislead investigators. Starting with animals allows them to refine their techniques without immediate risk."

"Could this escalate further?" Tee asked.

"Absolutely. If unchecked, the behaviour can progress to human victims. The thrill diminishes over time, pushing them to seek greater satisfaction. You said the girl was found posed? That's not random. That's part of the same progression."

Zak frowned. "So we're not dealing with someone who's snapped."

"No," Dr. Harper said firmly. "This has been brewing. For years, possibly."

Public Concern

News of the pattern began to leak, causing public concern. Pet owners were on edge, and community meetings were held to address safety.

Tee and Zak attended one such meeting, facing a crowd of anxious residents in a cold, echoing hall with folding chairs and stale coffee.

"We understand your fears," Tee addressed the gathering. "We're actively investigating and urge everyone to report any suspicious activity. We have increased patrols and are following new leads."

A woman raised her hand. "My neighbour's cat went missing last week. We found its collar near the woods. Should I report that?"

"Absolutely," Zak said. "Please speak to one of our team after the meeting. Every piece of information helps."

"Are our children safe?" someone called from the back.

Tee paused. "We don't believe the perpetrator is targeting anyone in particular. But it's always better to be cautious. Walk in pairs. Stay in lit areas. And if something feels wrong, report it."

The room didn't feel reassured. But they hadn't come looking for comfort. They'd come for truth.

A Breakthrough

Back at the station, a call came in. A jogger had discovered a freshly mutilated cat near the park. Tee and Zak rushed to the scene.

The body was positioned unnaturally, with symbols drawn nearby, carefully etched into the dirt.

"He's getting bolder," Tee observed, kneeling beside the corpse. "Leaving messages now."

Zak photographed the scene, noting the precision of the cuts and the placement of the body.

"This isn't just about killing. It's a message."

They bagged the evidence carefully, including some hair fibres and fragments of burned paper nearby, like remnants of a ritual.

Connecting the Dots

Back at the station, the symbols were cross-referenced with known occult and gang signs but returned no obvious matches. However, a linguist with the Met's special crimes division identified them as ancient Norse runes, obscure ones, symbolising sacrifice, judgement, and power.

"He's creating a narrative," Tee mused. "In his mind, these acts have meaning."

"Or he's trying to build a mythology around himself," Zak added. "Killer as god."

They added this to the profile. Someone young. Educated. Local. Delusional, but ordered. A mix of control and performance.

The Next Step

Realising the urgency, they formed a dedicated task force, drawing in analysts, dog handlers, and digital forensics. Community intelligence was revisited, cold cases re-opened.

They began pulling files on individuals with a history of animal cruelty, focusing on those with prior charges within the mapped boundary.

One name stood out.

Daniel Ro, 24. Once considered a promising veterinary student at a mid-tier university, Daniel's academic trajectory veered off-course after a disturbing incident at age seventeen: he was found in his family's garage dissecting a neighbour's missing cat with crude surgical precision. When questioned, he was disturbingly calm, claiming it was for "educational purposes." The authorities issued a caution for animal cruelty there wasn't enough to press further charges at the time — but the event marked the beginning of a slow and troubling descent.

He dropped out of veterinary school after his first year, citing "philosophical differences" with the curriculum. Since then, he had remained largely on the fringes living at home with a reclusive mother, taking occasional work at a local pet crematorium, and gradually withdrawing from face-to-face interaction. His neighbours described him as "quiet," "odd," and "always watching." One even recalled him digging in the woods behind their estate late at night.

A deep dive into his online footprint painted a far darker picture.

Using various aliases most notably *SarkothRunes* and *VolurHexBorn,* Daniel had been a frequent contributor to obscure forums and subreddits focused on Norse mythology, esoteric ritualism, and the symbolic use of blood in pre-Christian rites. His posts were long, often rambling, but disturbingly articulate laced with references to ancient texts, runic magic, and the necessity of "sacrifice to restore balance."

Several posts fixated on the idea of "pain as purification," and the belief that certain individuals were "chosen by pattern" that their suffering, if properly ritualised, could open a "circle of power." He referenced "marking boundaries in blood," "aligning offerings to the moon's tide," and, repeatedly, "the keystone."

In one post, dated six weeks before Sarah Morgan's disappearance, he wrote under the pseudonym:
"The keystone must be pure and unaware. Chosen not for who they are, but for what they represent. If the blood sings right, the door opens."

Though not directly incriminating, the phrasing and timing drew intense scrutiny.

His obsession with control through pain both emotional and physical suggested a potential pathology. But the most unsettling aspect was the consistency in tone: Daniel wasn't writing to shock. He was explaining something he *believed.*

His last known address? Inside the ring. Just three streets from where Sarah had last been seen alive.

Surveillance and Discovery

They didn't move immediately. First, they watched.

Daniel Ro lived alone in a neglected two-storey terrace that backed onto woodland. Cameras captured him coming and going at odd hours, often carrying bags he never returned with. No visitors. No family.

Then, early one morning, a dog unit picked up a foul scent in the woodland behind his house. A shallow pit. Inside, a notebook wrapped in plastic.

The notebook contained lists. Names. Drawings. Runes. One name had been underlined repeatedly.
Sarah Holt.

Zak stared at it for a long time. "He wrote about her before she died."

Tee said nothing. Her jaw tightened.

The Raid

Armed with a warrant, they raided the property. The stench inside was overwhelming, decay masked under bleach and incense.

In the basement, they found a space that had clearly been prepared, a mattress on the floor, ropes, knives, and a red-painted circle scrawled onto the concrete.

It wasn't just a hideout. It was a ritual chamber.

Daniel Ro didn't resist. He sat in the living room, hands folded in his lap, watching the officers swarm in as if he'd been expecting them.

"Do you understand why you're being arrested?" Zak asked, as the cuffs went on.

Daniel smiled. "Ah I was wondering when you'd come knocking on my door. I've been watching this case, quite impressive really."

The Interrogation

The interview room was cold not just from the hum of the air conditioning, but from something deeper, something in the walls. It smelled faintly of bleach and coffee left too long in its pot. The lights above buzzed like insects, a faint tremor of white noise that seemed to get louder the longer you sat in it.

Daniel Rowe was already waiting when Tee and Zak entered. His wrists were loosely cuffed in front of him, fingers twitching idly against each other like he was counting beats no one else could hear. He didn't rise when they came in. Just watched. Head tilted slightly. A look of faint amusement playing across his pale face, like he was observing a piece of performance art.

He was too calm. Not per-formatively, so not the smug bravado of someone revelling in control but something worse. Resigned. Content. Like none of this surprised him.

Tee dropped the evidence file onto the metal table with a soft *thump*. Zak followed it with a spread of photos the woodland site, the runes, the dead animals twisted into unnatural shapes, Sarah Morgan's school portrait framed by grim black tape.

"Let's start with the basics," Zak said evenly. "Do you know Sarah Morgan?"

Daniel's eyes flicked to the photo. Just for a moment. Then away. "I've seen her face. After she died. The news. Headlines." He said it like it was an inconvenience.

Tee's voice was low but sharp. "Her name appears in your journal. Not just mentioned circled. Underlined. You called her the 'keystone.' Care to explain that?"

Daniel's jaw twitched. Not in guilt. In irritation. "You're misreading it," he said, voice tight. "You always do. You people. You think a symbol means confession. A metaphor equals guilt. That's not how it works."

"Then help us understand," Zak said, arms folded. Calm, but the tension in his shoulders betrayed him.

Daniel gave a small laugh. "I write to process thought. You ever try that, Detective? Get the noise out? It doesn't mean I acted on anything. The runes, the rituals it's all theoretical. Ancient symbology. Alignment. Power maps. But I didn't hurt her."

Zak raised an eyebrow. "So you're admitting to staging dead animals, painting in blood, burying them in ritualistic patterns but Sarah, somehow, is where your ethics kick in?"

Daniel's head snapped up. The calm cracked just for a breath. "I'd never hurt a human," he said. "Animals were… something else. I used them for channeling. Energy. I'm not proud of it. But Sarah? That wasn't me."

"You wrote about her *before* she died," Tee said.

Daniel looked up at her, something flickering in his eyes. "I wrote about the *pattern*. The idea of a centrepiece. A keystone. Someone who fits. I didn't name her. I didn't pick her. But when I saw her face on the news..." He trailed off.

Zak's voice dropped. "Then who did?"

Silence.

Daniel's lips twitched not a smile, not quite. Reverence.

"Whoever did it," he said finally, softly, "was brilliant."

The room shifted. The air changed. Zak froze, his pen mid-stroke above the notebook. Tee didn't blink.

Daniel leaned forward slightly. "The way her body was found. The alignment. The use of space, balance, ritual geometry that wasn't rage. It wasn't clumsy. It was... deliberate. Artful."

Tee's voice went cold. "You admire them?"

He didn't flinch. "You people make entire Netflix categories about serial killers. Don't pretend fascination isn't part of the job. Bundy. Dahmer. You study them because they *defy* normal human wiring. Not for the *what*, but for the *how*. Whoever did this they weren't panicked. They were precise. Controlled. That's… rare."

Zak's knuckles whitened on the table edge. "You sound like a fanboy."

Daniel finally smiled. "No. I sound like someone who recognises talent."

"Jesus," Zak muttered.

"I could never do what they did," Daniel continued, gaze glassy. "Not with that level of… grace. I'm impulsive. Messy. I tried to control it through ritual, through animal work, but I could never touch something like *that*. Whoever they are, they're beyond me. I study patterns. I don't create them."

Tee leaned forward, tone sharp and slicing. "You said 'patterns.' So you think Sarah's death is part of something larger?"

Daniel looked between them, and then, maddeningly, gave a lazy shrug. "Maybe. Maybe not. I said *I* didn't choose her. Doesn't mean no one did."

Zak straightened. "Are you saying you know who did this?"

Daniel met his eyes directly. "I'm saying *you* don't."

Zak's jaw tightened. "The animal mutilations. The cat killings. That was you. You served time for that."

Daniel nodded once. "Six months. Prison. Therapy. Probation. All ticked off. But ask yourself something, Detective… look at the timeline. The way the girl was found. The symbols. The condition of the body. Doesn't match, does it? I'm chaos. She was order. And no, you don't get both in the same person."

Tee narrowed her eyes. "Are you saying they're not connected?"

"I'm saying," Daniel said slowly, "maybe you've been chasing the wrong narrative. The cat killer and the girl's murderer? You think they're the same person. That's convenient. Easy. But convenient stories blind you to harder truths."

Zak leaned forward, voice taut. "What are you implying?"

Daniel's gaze glinted. "Come on, detective. I shouldn't have to do your job for you."

Then he pushed back his chair slightly, as far as the cuffs allowed, and gave a theatrical sigh. "Are we done now? You've properly ruined my evening."

Tee stared at him, something cold and coiled twisting in her gut. She had wanted this to be over. To walk away knowing the town's bogeyman was the right monster.

But something about Daniel's words hung in the air like static. He was still dangerous, still unhinged but maybe not in the way they needed him to be.

His journal, retrieved during a search of his bedroom, contained hand-drawn runes, anatomical sketches of both animals and humans, and references to Sarah's name underlined, circled, with cryptic notes like "pulse in the pattern" and "the girl by the water."

There were no overt confessions.
Just an overwhelming sense that Daniel Ro had been preparing for something, something he claimed he didn't commit, but clearly anticipated.

Whether he was a disturbed fantasist or a key witness to something even darker… was now the question.

12

They don't see the whole picture yet.
Not even close.

They're still stumbling through shadows, hoping for light.
But this isn't their game, it's mine. I set the rules. I decide
the pace. And they're already playing, whether they admit
it or not.

Daniel was never meant to be anything more than a decoy.
A distraction. I knew he'd draw attention eventually. The
way he flaunted his fascination, the journals, the dead
animals, the symbols, it was always going to catch
someone's eye. But he wasn't dangerous.

Not really.

He wanted to be me. And that made him useful.

Let them pull him in. Let them dissect his every word,
hoping he'll confess to something he didn't do.
Meanwhile, the real game is moving forward. Quietly.
Perfectly.

I went back to the quarry last night, the old one behind the
ridge where the kids used to hang out after school, where
they smoked cheap cigarettes and carved promises into

tree trunks. So many names over the years. So many "forevers."

It's ironic, isn't it? How easily forever breaks.
I chose one of those trees. One still scarred with faded initials and hearts. And beneath it, I carved my message, slow, deliberate strokes with the hunting knife I keep wrapped in cloth under the floorboards. The blade is clean, always. Honed to a whisper.

One by one you'll fall.

No signature. No need.
They'll know.

I could almost see it playing out in my mind as I walked away, early morning light filtering through the leaves, a dog walker pausing, leaning closer, the sharp intake of breath when they read the words. The phone call. The flashing blue lights. And blondie detectives face as she arrives at the scene, her brow furrowed, her jaw tight.

*

Later that morning, I walk through town. Blending in is easy. I've always been good at it. The trick is to be forgettable, not invisible, just *unremarkable*. Smiling when someone glances your way. Helping an old man lift his shopping into the boot of his car. People remember kindness. But they don't *watch* it.

I move through the streets like smoke. Drifting. Listening.

They're talking about Sarah now, still unsure what to call what happened to her. Tragedy? Accident? Murder? That word's growing louder. Sharper. No one says it outright yet, but it's there, coiled in the back of their throats.

My pulse doesn't change. My breath stays steady.

But I smile.

I pass the park bench where Emma Shaw is sitting. She doesn't see me. Her head's bent, hands trembling slightly as she checks her phone. Another message, probably. Another warning. I've sent three now. Just enough to make her wonder. Just enough to keep her up at night.
She thinks it's a prank. She *wants* it to be a prank.

But the crack is there. I can see it in her posture, the way her shoulders curl inward, like she's trying to shrink into herself. Like she already knows she's being watched.

Good.
She was never innocent. None of them were.

They laughed while she cried. They whispered when they thought no one could hear. They turned the other way, let her unravel, then moved on like she'd never mattered. Like she hadn't been part of them.

They broke her.

And now I'm breaking them.
Piece by piece.

*

Back home, I lay everything out on the table. The notebook is almost full now, page after page of names, dates, observations. I've rewritten "the list" so many times it's etched into my memory. But I still like the ritual of it. The physical act of writing. The finality of ink.

Maya Brooks.
Tom Grant.
Ben Carter.
Emma Shaw.

I stare at the name at the top, in darker ink, pressed so hard the pen nearly tore the page:

Lily Shaw.

She was the beginning. The wound they all helped create. And I promised her someone would make them feel it. All of it.

I close the notebook and set it aside.

There's one more step tonight. One more message to deliver. Something a little closer. A little bolder. They're starting to connect the dots now. The map. The symbols. The escalation.

Good.

Let them find patterns. Let them theorise, scramble, panic.

But while they're chasing lines on a wall, I'll be setting the next piece in motion.

One by one.

They'll fall.

Part Three

13

Emma

The fight started over nothing, a stupid, offhand comment about Maya's choice of university, but it was just the match to a fire that had been smouldering for weeks.

We were all pretending, going through the motions of friendship. Sitting outside our usual café on the high street, sun glinting off iced drinks and phone screens, trying to hold onto the version of ourselves that had existed before everything fractured.

But it was too late.

Tom flicked a piece of paper from the table, his jaw tight. "Not all of us can afford to mess around for three years doing Performing Arts, you know."

The words dropped like a stone in the middle of the table. Maya's head snapped up, her mouth parting in disbelief. "Excuse me?" she said, her voice sharp, incredulous.

Tom didn't blink. "You heard me. Some of us are actually trying to get jobs after all this. Useful jobs."

Maya pushed her chair back slightly, her face pale beneath her usual foundation. "Right. Because your business degree is going to save the world?"

"Because it's practical," he snapped.

Ben looked up from his drink, trying, and failing, to act like he hadn't been watching this unfold. "Can we not do this?" he said weakly. "Seriously, we're all on edge. Let's just—"

"On edge?" Maya repeated, turning to him. "That's your contribution? Maybe if Tom wasn't being a complete ass —"

"I'm just saying what everyone's thinking," Tom cut in, voice rising. "It's always been about Maya. Her shows, her drama productions, her big future."

I tried to speak. I really did. I opened my mouth, something about stress and how we were all scared and this wasn't about Maya's drama degree. But the words dried up before they could take form.

Because none of it would have helped. The tension wasn't about university choices. It wasn't about careers. It was about fear, the kind that crept under your skin and made everything tighter, sharper, more fragile.

Lately, it felt like everything could break.

And Lily… Lily just sat there.

Apart.

She was at the table with us, but she might as well have been somewhere else entirely. Her sleeves were pulled over her hands, and she was drawing spirals on a napkin with a dull biro, so focused that I wondered if she could even hear us anymore.

When Maya stood up, rattling the table, Lily flinched but didn't look up.

"I'm done," Maya said, voice shaking. "I don't need this. Not from you."

Tom rolled his eyes, but there was something brittle in the gesture. "Go on then, storm off. That's what you're best at. And the Oscar goes too…"

Maya spun on her heel and stalked away down the high street. I watched her go, part of me wanting to follow, part of me too drained to move.

"Jesus," Ben muttered, running his hand through his hair. "What the hell is happening to us?"

The silence that followed was the worst part. Thick, awkward, almost accusatory.

"We're not okay," I said finally, my voice quieter than I expected.

Tom snorted, as if that was stating the obvious. "Took you long enough."

Lily finally looked up.

Her eyes were dark, tired in a way that didn't make sense for someone who'd been in bed by ten every night. She didn't say anything, didn't offer a joke or a word of comfort like she used to. She just stared at me for a beat too long and then turned her gaze back to the napkin, continuing her spirals like they were the only thing tethering her to the present.

And in that moment, it hit me like a wave.

We weren't the same.

We hadn't been the same in weeks.
Ever since Sarah.

Even before she'd been found, before the news reports and the vigils and the whispered questions about whether we really knew her, even before all that, something had shifted. We had started to drift. Little things. Less time spent together. Shorter conversations. More silences filled with scrolling instead of talking.

Now it felt like we were standing on the wreckage of something we used to love and trying to convince ourselves it was still whole.

I paid for my drink and left without saying much more. Ben nodded slightly at me as I stood, like he understood.

Tom was already tapping something on his phone, jaw still clenched.

And Lily? She was still drawing spirals. Tiny, tight circles, coiling inward and inward like she was trying to trap herself inside them.

Outside, the high street buzzed with life, parents dragging tired toddlers home, couples shopping for picnics, groups of teenagers laughing too loudly as they passed.

It felt like I was walking through another world. One that didn't know, or didn't care, about the slow implosion of ours.

I walked for a while. Past the corner shop we used to meet at before school, past the alley behind the gym where Ben once kissed Maya and then pretended it hadn't happened.

Past the skatepark where Tom used to sit on the fence and throw M&Ms at us for fun.

Everything carried memories, like landmines.

I ended up at the old bridge, the one that crossed the river and led into the quarry. We'd carved our names into the wooden railing years ago, a pact, back when forever meant something. I found the letters there, faded but still visible. E, B, M, T, L

Us.

And underneath a new carving

One by one you'll fall.

My heart dropped, I felt a wave of nausea, my heading started spinning and I could hear my blood gushing around in my head like a tsunami waiting to hit.

Someone was watching.Waiting.

I began to shiver uncontrollably, even though the air was warm.

I turned back. I didn't want to walk into the woods. Not alone. I shouldn't be here, I had to leave right now. They knew I would come, that I would see this new carving, I was a target, we all were and I'd been lured into their trap.

As I retraced my steps, I tried to convince myself that the group would be fine. That this was just stress. Exams. University offers. The aftermath of tragedy.

But I knew better.

This wasn't just drifting.

This was splintering.

And I wasn't sure we'd come back together again.

When I got home, I found a note shoved through the letterbox. No envelope. No address. Just a piece of lined paper, folded once.

My stomach dropped.
I opened it slowly, heart hammering.

You pretend you're innocent.
But you know what you did.
One by one.

I sat on the stairs, the note trembling in my hands.

At first, I'd convinced myself it was a joke. A prank. Someone being cruel. I suspected Tom initially, he could be cruel, he's been so chilled and unbothered about everything thats been going on.

But now I wasn't so sure. Surely Tom wouldn't be this cruel, but I know he has a nasty side, I've seen it.

Something or someone wanted us to pay.

And deep down, I was starting to think we deserved it.

This was the push I needed, I needed to go to the police, they needed to see these notes. The gang would never speak to me again, the police are going to ask questions and then want to talk to them. I don't have anything to hide, I didn't do anything wrong. I haven't done anything.

14

DI Tee and DC Zak

The interrogation room was silent now, the air thick with the residue of Daniel's unsettling admiration for the killer's precision. DI Tee sat alone, the dim light casting elongated shadows across the table. Daniel's words echoed in his mind: "Whoever did this... they were brilliant. Surgical. I could never achieve that level of perfection." The statement was less a confession and more a chilling commendation.

Tee reviewed the evidence laid out before him: photographs of the crime scene, forensic reports, and Daniel's background. The victim, Sarah, had been found with precise incisions, each cut deliberate, almost artistic. Daniel, a former medical student turned recluse, had the knowledge but lacked the motive, or so it seemed.

He recalled Daniel's demeanour during the interrogation: calm, composed, and disturbingly fascinated. There was no sign of remorse, only a deep appreciation for the killer's methodology. It was as if Daniel saw the murder as a masterpiece, not a crime.

Tee knew she needed to delve deeper into Daniel's psyche. She arranged for a psychological evaluation, hoping to uncover any latent tendencies or obsessions that might link him to the crime. In the meantime, she instructed her team, including her partner DC Zak, to re-examine Daniel's past, looking for any connections to similar cases or unexplained incidents.

As the investigation progressed, Tee couldn't shake the feeling that Daniel was more involved than he let on. The admiration, the knowledge, the detachment, it all pointed to someone who was either the killer or dangerously close to them. The line between observer and participant was blurring, and Tee was determined to find the truth before another life was claimed. Or maybe that's what the killer wanted us to think? To throw us off the scent.

Later that evening, as Tee sifted through the case files in his office, a knock at the door interrupted his thoughts. He looked up to see Emma standing there, her face pale and eyes wide with a mix of fear and determination.

"Detective, " she said, her voice trembling slightly, "I think you need to see these."

She stepped into the room, holding a stack of notes bound together with a rubber band. Tee gestured for her to sit, and she handed him the bundle.

"They were left for me," Emma explained. "Anonymous notes. Threatening, cryptic. I didn't think much of them at first, but after Sarah… I can't ignore them anymore."

Tee carefully examined the notes. The handwriting was neat, almost meticulous. Each message was brief but chilling:

"You pretend you're innocent."
"But you know what you did."
"One by one."

The phrases mirrored the killer's modus operandi, taunting, psychological manipulation, a sense of impending doom. These notes were more than just threats; they were a direct link to the murderer.

"Emma, why didn't you come forward with these earlier?" Tee asked, trying to keep her tone calm.

"I was scared," she admitted. "I thought it was some sick joke. But now, with everything that's happened, I realise it's serious."

Tee nodded, understanding the weight of her fear. "You've done the right thing by bringing them to me now. We'll analyse these notes for fingerprints, DNA, anything that can help us identify the sender."

She paused, considering the implications. "Emma, do you have any idea why you would be sent these notes?

She shook her head.

"Emma you're not in trouble, we just need to know if anything has happened that would make someone want to send you these." Tee said sympathetically

"Not that I know of. But we've all been on edge lately. The tension, the fights... it's like something's tearing us apart."

"One more question, has anyone else received any messages like this? Any of your friends?" Tee asked.

Emma shook her head and said she didn't know.

"Thank you for coming forward," she said sincerely. "We'll do everything we can to keep you safe and find out who's behind this."

As Emma left the office, Tee turned her attention back to the notes. This new evidence was a breakthrough, a tangible connection to the killer's mindset. The game had changed, and the stakes were higher than ever.

*

The next few days passed in a blur. Tee and Zak worked around the clock, analysing the notes, cross-referencing them with Daniel's background, and digging deeper into the lives of Sarah, Emma, and the people who surrounded them. Every clue seemed to take them in different directions, each piece of evidence more confusing than the last.

The forensic team's analysis of the notes had returned with few results. No fingerprints. No DNA. But something had been discovered: the paper used for the notes had been purchased from a local stationery shop, a place frequented by a number of people from Sarah's circle. It wasn't much, but it was a lead. It could have been anyone, but they could deduce that it's someone local.

Tee had also arranged for Daniel's psychological evaluation, but it came back inconclusive. The doctor reported that Daniel exhibited no signs of psychopathy, no abnormal fixation on violence or death. But Tee wasn't convinced. The admiration Daniel had expressed for the killer's work felt too specific, too calculated. It wasn't simply a fascination; it was envy. The killer's precision was something Daniel seemed to long for.

Yet, as the investigation deepened, a sense of unease began to settle over Tee. She had come to a harsh conclusion: Daniel was not the killer, but the killer might be someone even closer to the case, someone who was toying with them all like puppets on strings.

DC Zak leaned against the whiteboard, arms crossed, eyes narrowed as he scanned the photos again. "I know Daniel's a convenient suspect," he said, his voice low but steady, "but we're too focused on him because he's weird, not because the evidence fits. The cuts, the precision, that's not just rage or impulse. That's training. This is someone who knows anatomy, someone who could be hell, *should be* a doctor. We're looking for someone with control."

Tee knew he was right, but something still wasn't adding up, the cats, the notes, Sarah. There were too many things too consider, but she knew time was running out.

*

It was late one night when Tee received another call from Emma. Her voice was frantic, urgent.

"Detective Tee, you need to come to my house," she said. "Something... something's happened."

Tee didn't hesitate. She grabbed her jacket and rushed out the door, his mind racing. As he drove through the darkened streets, his thoughts spun out of control. Was Emma in danger? Had the killer found her?

When she arrived, Emma was standing outside her house, shaking. Her face was pale, and her eyes were wide with fear.

"Emma, what's happened?" Tee asked, her voice laced with concern.

"I... I don't know how to explain it," she said, her voice trembling. "The notes. There's a new one."

She handed Tee a crumpled piece of paper, her hands unsteady. She took it and read the chilling message:
"You're closer than you think."

For a moment, Tee stood frozen, the implications of the note crashing down on him. The killer had been in plain sight the whole time. Daniel wasn't the killer; he was the puppet or even a mask. The killer had been manipulating him, Emma, and everyone involved. The sudden realisation hit Tee like a bolt of lightning, Daniel had been a pawn in the killer's twisted game, an unwitting accomplice, or perhaps just a mirror reflecting the true nature of the killer's obsession.

The game wasn't about admiration. It was about control.

Tee looked up at Emma, her mind working rapidly.

*

Back in Tee's office, the pieces began to fall into place. The killer wasn't Daniel; but they were after Emma. The notes were meant to unsettle her, to make her question her own innocence. The killer had been setting up a scenario where everyone around her would feel complicit in Sarah's death, whether they were or not. Tee had seen this before: the killer's need to force their victims to confront their own guilt, to question everything they thought they knew.

Tee paced the room, her mind racing. If Daniel wasn't the killer, then who was? The connection between the killer and Sarah, and by extension Emma, was clearer now. The killer had been moving through the circle, picking at the fractures in their relationships, isolating them one by one.

Then the final piece clicked. Tee had been so focused on the idea that Daniel might be the killer that she had missed the simplest explanation. The killer was someone who knew them intimately, who had access to their secrets and their fears.

The realisation hit Tee like a punch to the gut. The killer was someone from Sarah's life, someone who had been watching, waiting, manipulating all along.

And the notes had been the key all along. Each message had been a challenge, a taunt meant to force someone into a corner.

*

Tee stood in front of the mirror in her office, the fluorescent lights above casting a harsh, clinical glow across her face. Her reflection looked back at her pale, drawn, eyes rimmed with exhaustion and something else just beneath the surface: fury.

She barely recognised herself anymore.

Dark shadows clung beneath her eyes, the kind that concealer couldn't cover, the kind that settled in when adrenaline became a constant and sleep was nothing but a memory. Her blazer hung looser on her frame than it had a month ago, shoulders tense, jaw set in a way that had become second nature. Every inch of her body ached not from injury, but from relentless, gnawing tension. The pressure never eased. Not when she was off-duty. Not even in her sleep.

Because she *wasn't* off-duty. Not really. Not since Sarah Morgan's body had been found with ritualistic precision, not since the first whispers of something calculated something evil had crawled out from under the surface of this town.

She splashed water on her face from the sink, gripping the edge of the basin as she breathed slowly, deliberately, trying to find a piece of herself again beneath the noise. She could still hear Daniel Rowe's voice echoing in her skull calm, cold, admiring.

"It was art. Something beyond me."
A part of her wanted to scream.

This wasn't theory. This wasn't academic.

This was a girl a *child* murdered, carefully, intimately. And someone out there thought of it as art.

She stared at her reflection again and saw the tightness in her throat mirrored in her expression the way her mouth pressed into a line, the way her eyes were bloodshot from too many late nights reading case files, watching grainy CCTV footage frame by frame, cross-referencing journals and timelines until everything blurred.

This job had always demanded sacrifice, but this case *this one* felt like it had reached inside her and taken something she didn't know she'd put on the table.

She used to trust her instincts. Used to believe that if you worked hard enough, paid attention to the cracks, justice followed. But now? She felt like she was drowning in doubt second-guessing her every move, the guilt mounting over every missed detail, every hour that passed without a new lead.

But something had shifted.

The killer had revealed themselves not by name, not openly but in symbolism, in control, in the way they were manipulating the story from the shadows. They weren't hiding anymore. They were playing. Leaving threads behind like breadcrumbs, daring her to follow.

And she *would*.

She pulled her shoulders back, her spine straightening as she ran a hand through her hair. The fatigue didn't vanish, but it settled tight and focused. Controlled.

She was done playing defence.

She wasn't going to let them write this story.

Not this time.

Tee turned away from the mirror, her steps slow but steady as she walked back toward her desk littered with photos, notes, evidence tags. She stared down at the map with all its pins and threads and markings, and felt something ignite in her chest.

Resolve.

They wanted to make this personal?

Fine.

They had no idea what she was capable of when it *was* personal.

And she wasn't stopping until they were caught or until she broke herself trying.

Whichever came first.

*

Meanwhile, DC Zak was poring over the evidence back at the station, the reports and notes spread out before him. He too felt the weight of their investigation bearing down on him. But something was off. His instincts told him that they were on the edge of something major, something darker than they had ever expected.

15

It's almost time.

I watched them today, watched their argument explode like a rotten fruit bursting open. The tension had been there for weeks. It had started off small, so subtle that no one even noticed. The subtle slights, the little jabs, the snide comments. A snicker here, an eye-roll there. That's how it always begins, doesn't it? Small enough to be ignored but building, slowly growing, until something tips it over the edge. It's like a slow boil, a rising pressure beneath the surface, just waiting for a spark.

And today, I was the spark.

It was almost too easy. All it took was one simple comment. Just the right thing at the right time. The kind of thing they would say to each other in their most vulnerable moments. When they think no one's listening, when they think the air is thick with comfort and security. That's when you say it. That's when you let it slip. And then, the floodgates open.

I could see the tension in their eyes even before the first words were said. The resentment that had been building up for so long, something dark that neither of them was willing to admit, was finally bubbling to the surface. A storm was coming, and I was the wind behind it, coaxing it into full force.

Their argument exploded in a way that was almost beautiful. It was loud, sharp, and angry, and for a moment, the world around them seemed to fade. I was there, of course, always watching, but for them, the rest of the world ceased to exist. They were in their bubble, spinning in their conflict, until it shattered. They said things they couldn't take back, things they would regret, things they couldn't even understand they meant, but the damage was done.

What they didn't know was that it didn't matter. It didn't matter if they regretted it or not. Because by the time they realised the truth, it would be far too late.

I had been preparing for this moment, this final ignition, for so long. It wasn't just about watching them fight. No, that was only the beginning. The real game was far more complex. It wasn't just about watching; it was about guiding, steering them down the path I'd already laid out for them.

They were pieces on a chessboard, and they had no idea who was pulling the strings.

*

After the argument, I saw the way they separated, each retreating into their own thoughts, their own heads. I followed them, though they didn't know. The world was quieter now, like a moment of calm after a storm. But it was only a temporary silence. The tension was still thick in the air, hanging like smoke, ready to suffocate.

The moment had come. It was time for the next step.

I approached Tom when he was distracted, when he was still in his own thoughts, confused by what had just happened. His face was flushed with anger, his eyes still wild from the heat of the argument. He didn't notice me slip the next clue into his backpack. A simple piece of paper. A tiny scrap that would set everything in motion. He would find it later, when he was home, alone.

It was a simple message. A simple message that would feel like a death sentence to him when he saw it. The words would echo in his mind long after he read them.

"You're next."

It didn't need to be anything more. That was the beauty of it. Just a few words, just a whisper of the inevitable. Tom wouldn't find it immediately. It wouldn't be until later, when he was at home, sitting alone in his room. Maybe when the house was quiet, when the lights flickered just a little too long, or when the sound of his own breathing was all he could hear. That was when the fear would settle in. When the shadows in his room felt just a little too thick, a little too alive.

I didn't need to make it obvious. In fact, the less obvious it was, the more effective it would be. It would sit there, nestled in his bag, waiting for the perfect moment. Tom would be carrying it around with him for hours, unaware of the message tucked away in the folds of his life. But when he finally found it, when his hands trembled as he unfolded it, it would hit him hard. Harder than anything else.

I already knew what would happen.

The panic would start small, just a slight tightening in his chest, a subtle knot in his stomach. But then the thoughts would begin. The thoughts that there was nowhere to run, no one to help, no way to escape. It would eat away at him, little by little. The darkness would seep in. The shadows would grow larger. The silence of his home, once comforting, would feel like a suffocating void.

And then, when he thought he couldn't take it any longer, I would be there. Right at the moment he cracked.

*

I could almost hear the fear in his breath, the way it would hitch in his throat as the reality set in. Tom would lie in his bed, staring at the ceiling, listening to the creaks of the house settling, wondering if it was all just a nightmare. He would wonder if anyone else was in the house with him. Was he being watched? Was there someone just outside his window, waiting for the right moment?

The fear would burrow under his skin. It would twist its way through him, pulling his thoughts into a spiral. He would question every sound, every shadow. And when he finally realised there was nowhere to run, that there was nothing left to do but face the truth, that's when he would start to break.

And I would be there, watching.
Just like I watched her.

*

I can still see her face clearly in my mind, every detail burned into my memory. Sarah. The way she knew this was it for her. The way the single tear rolled down her face. The way she thought, somehow, that there was a chance, that someone would come to her rescue.

I remember the desperation in her eyes, cracking with the weight of her own fear. She thought they would save her.

She thought they were her friends, her allies. But that was her mistake. That was always her mistake.

They didn't care. They never did. But I care, I have always cared and now I have ended her pain.

This is just about Sarah, they watched as Lily suffered. They looked away when she cried. They pretended to care when it suited them, but when it came down to it, they left her to die. I watched it all unfold, each one of them complicit in their own way. But I was patient. I had time. I knew what I had to do.

They were all so predictable, weren't they? They all thought they were above it. They thought they were immune. But I knew the truth. I knew they couldn't outrun themselves. They couldn't outrun the darkness they carried inside them. The guilt. The shame. The lies.

I waited. I watched. And when they thought they were safe, when they thought they could breathe again, that's when I moved in.

And now, I was going to do it all over again.

*

Tom would break. I was sure of it. He would start to see the world differently, and his perception of safety, of normalcy, would fade. The walls would close in on him. The isolation would be unbearable. And he would begin to wonder what had brought him to this point. What had led him here? Was it something he had done? Someone he had hurt?

The fear would gnaw at him. He would try to deny it, of course. He would try to push it away, tell himself it was just a joke, just a prank. But that wouldn't last. The fear was already inside him, curling in his gut, reaching into his chest. It would settle in and fester. And by the time I came for him, he would already be halfway broken.

That's how it worked. The fear was the beginning. The fear was the invitation.

And the rest was inevitable.

*

I let the thought of him, of his eventual collapse, linger for a moment. The anticipation made the whole process so much sweeter. The way they would try to resist, the way they would fight back in the beginning thinking that they could beat me, outsmart me. But they never do.

Just like Sarah never did.

I remember when she had stood there in the corridor that day, clutching her books like they could shield her, eyes darting for a teacher, a friend, anyone. She still believed back then, believed that if she said the right thing, someone would step in, that kindness could still win. But no one came. The sniggers echoed louder than any help. The whispers cut deeper than the names. And in that moment, as her shoulders sank and her voice faltered, the truth settled in her eyes no one was coming. No one cared enough to stop it. The world was full of promises, yes, but most of them were already broken. And she had become just another crack in the foundation.

And now, Tom would become just another victim in the long line of them.

By the time I came for him, there wouldn't be a fight left. He would already be halfway to the edge. He would already be halfway broken.

Just like they broke her.

16

Emma

The call came just after midnight. I was half-asleep, drifting somewhere between a dream and that cold tug of wakefulness. The vibration of my phone on the nightstand startled me more than the sound itself. When I saw Maya's name on the screen, something inside me twisted. I knew before I even answered that this wasn't just some casual late-night chat.

"Tom's missing," she said. Her voice wasn't just shaking. It was raw. Stripped down to nerves.

I sat bolt upright, the sheets tangling around my legs. "What do you mean, missing?"

"He didn't come home," Maya said quickly. "His mum called me. She thought maybe he was with us, hanging out, or… I don't know. She's freaking out. She found his phone charger still plugged in. His bed's untouched."

I pushed the hair out of my face. "Maybe he's just at a mate's house. Maybe he crashed somewhere and forgot to —"

"No," she cut me off. "He texted me around eight. Said he felt weird. That someone was following him."

I froze. The words hit like a slap, like being dunked in ice water. I couldn't respond at first. Couldn't even process what I was hearing.

Because I've felt that feeling. It's like Sarah all over again. According to her friends, she had said the same thing. They all brushed it off and said it was paranoia.

And then she was gone.

Now it was Tom.

Lily and I have both had the same feeling, does that mean that we have been followed? That someone is stalking us? This is too coincidental now, this is serious, we are not safe.

My voice cracked when I finally spoke. "Did he say who?"

"No. Just that he felt off. Like someone was behind him, but when he looked back, there was no one." Maya's breath caught. "He said it felt like the air changed. Like it was watching him."

My mouth had gone dry.

"I'm going to his place," I said, already swinging my legs out of bed, already grabbing my hoodie from the chair. "I'll meet you there."

*

The street was lit in that eerie, sodium-orange glow that made everything feel both too exposed and not visible enough. I arrived just after Maya. The front door was open. Too wide. Like a wound in the night.

Tom's mum was in the living room, crumpled on the edge of the sofa, his jacket in her hands like a child clutching a security blanket. She didn't even look up as I walked in, just kept staring at the door, as if willing him to walk through it.

There were two police officers standing in the hall, speaking in low, carefully modulated tones to each other. They acknowledged us with a brief glance but didn't stop their work. They were checking his last phone location, interviewing neighbours. They'd probably already walked the block, already questioned the usual suspects. But it felt like routine. Like this was just the beginning of something they didn't yet understand.

Tom's room was upstairs. Still messy. Still his. Shoes on the floor, guitar pick on the nightstand, half-drunk can of energy drink next to his gaming headset. The mundane normality of it made everything worse. Like he'd just walked out to the shop and hadn't come back.

But we all knew it wasn't that.

Maya stood next to me, arms wrapped around her stomach like she was holding herself together. I kept expecting her to speak, to fill the silence with the kind of frantic energy she was known for, but she didn't. She was too still.

Then someone else arrived. Ben. Pale, shaking, eyes darting around like he didn't want to be here, didn't want to be anywhere.

"I got a message," he said.

"What message?" I asked.

He pulled out his phone, and I saw the screen lit up with a photo. My stomach lurched.

It was a shot of Tom's street, taken from behind a bush. His front door in the frame. The caption read:

"Too late."

Maya gasped and turned away. Ben swore under his breath and sat heavily on Tom's desk chair, the wheels squeaking.

It was happening again.

Sarah. Now Tom. One by one.

The whisper at the back of my mind, the one I'd been trying to ignore, now screamed: This isn't over. This is just starting.

*

The police questioned us all. One by one.

What time did you last speak to him?
Did he say anything unusual?
Has Tom ever talked about hurting himself?

That last question made Maya snap. Her jaw clenched, fists curling at her sides.

"He didn't run away, okay?" she spat. "He didn't just decide to disappear. Something happened. Someone did something."

The officer didn't flinch, just nodded and scribbled something down. Another detective glanced at the hallway, then murmured something to the lead investigator. They asked us to step outside while they spoke to Tom's mum again. She didn't argue didn't even seem to hear them. She just nodded slowly, still clutching Tom's jacket in both hands like it could bring him back. Her eyes were vacant, ringed with red.

Tom's mum suddenly turned from the window, her voice hoarse but sharp as broken glass. "You," she snapped, eyes locking on Maya. "You're a nasty girl. I never liked you. I told Tom you were no good always dragging him into things, always talking back. I never wanted you seeing my son."

Maya froze, her face hardening, but something flickered behind her eyes something close to shame. No one said a word. The silence that followed felt colder than summer air.

We drifted into the back garden. Cold air hit our faces like a slap. None of us said anything at first. We just stood there three teenagers huddled under the weight of something far too big for any of us to name. The patio stones were damp beneath our feet, the garden strangely quiet, like even the birds knew not to interrupt.

Ben sat on the edge of the garden bench, rubbing his thumb over the edge of his thumbnail until it bled. Maya paced. I leaned against the shed wall, arms crossed, stomach churning.

"He wasn't himself lately. Tom. He was... quieter. Twitchy." She said.

"He said he wasn't sleeping," Ben added, eyes fixed on the ground. "Said he kept waking up and feeling like there was someone in the room."

I nodded slowly. "Sarah said the same thing. Before she died."

That made everyone look up.

"Apparently she told her friends," I said, swallowing hard, "that someone was following her. That she could feel them watching. That they were leaving her notes. Weird ones. She was scared."

Ben stared at me, his face pale. "And they didn't believe her."

Maya folded her arms tightly over her chest. "Her friends thought she was spiralling. Told her she needed therapy. Told her it was in her head."

"But what if it wasn't?" I whispered. My voice cracked on the last word. "What if she was right?"

The question hung in the air, sharp and unforgiving.
No one answered.

Because we were all thinking the same thing all tracing the same jagged line from Sarah to Tom. All remembering how quick we were to dismiss the strange. The uncomfortable. How we laughed off the notes, the paranoia, the signs. How we never once thought to dig deeper.

And now he was gone.

I looked around at the others. Maya's face was stony but her hands trembled. Ben's shoulders had curled in on themselves like he was trying to disappear. Ben wouldn't meet anyone's eyes.

The guilt sat heavy in the pit of my stomach, tightening with every second.

We didn't believe Sarah.

And now it was happening again.

What if this was never over?

Who was next?

*

Back inside, the air was stifling, thick with the smell of stale coffee and sweat, and something else none of us could name. An officer called me over, his expression unreadable as he held up a small evidence bag.

"Does this belong to any of you?" he asked.

Inside was a single folded piece of paper.

My blood turned to ice.

Even through the plastic, I knew what it was, the same creamy paper, the same impossibly neat handwriting, like it had been written with a ruler. I didn't need to read it. I already knew what it said. But I read it anyway.

You left her there.

The words hit like a punch to the gut. The floor didn't feel real anymore. I had to grip the edge of the kitchen counter to keep from sliding to the ground. My vision blurred at the edges, a sharp ringing in my ears.

Maya stepped closer, her eyes locked on the note. "It's the same, isn't it?" she said flatly. "Same handwriting as Emma's notes."

The officer didn't answer, but he didn't need to. The tight set of his jaw was answer enough.

Ben ran a hand through his hair, pacing. "Who the hell is doing this?" he asked, his voice rough, almost breaking. "Why now?"

But none of us spoke.

Because deep down, in that aching space just below our ribcages, we were all thinking the same thing.

This wasn't random.

This was deliberate.

Calculated.

Personal.

I opened my mouth, heart hammering, words slipping out before I could stop them. "Guys, do you think this has anything to do with—"

"Em, just stop talking." Maya's voice was sharp, dangerous. She moved fast, stepping in front of me, eyes wide and furious. "This isn't the time. The police are crawling around, are you actually insane?"

Her reaction was too fast, too rehearsed.

Guilt prickled up my neck like static.

I shut my mouth. I knew I'd said too much.

We'd made a promise.

We would never talk about that night.

And now the past was crawling out of the shadows.

One note at a time.

*

9 Months Earlier

Sarah

I only came to St Cedars for the art department.

My old school didn't offer Art A-Level, and I remember thinking it was a sign when I saw the St Cedars prospectus bold, bright, promising creativity and independence. I imagined studios with tall windows, the smell of paint and paper, teachers who saw the world like I did. I thought it would be my place. I knew a lot of people there, so it wouldn't be difficult to fit in.

I didn't expect to be a target for them.
Emma. Tom. Ben. Maya. Lily.

They were the first people I spoke to loud, confident, always surrounded by people who laughed too hard at things that weren't funny. They introduced themselves before the first lesson even started, Emma asking if I was "new new" or just someone they hadn't noticed before. It was meant as a joke. I laughed, even though it stung. I mean we had met before, but never really spoke.

At first, I thought they liked me.

Tom would say hi in the corridor. Maya asked to see my sketchbook once. Lily complimented my necklace. It all felt easy like maybe I'd found the kind of people I'd always watched from a distance but never belonged to.

That lasted maybe two weeks.

Then came the comments.

Little ones, sharp as paper cuts.

"That's what you're wearing?"
"Is that how you always do your hair?"
"Your sketchbook's... brave."
They said it with smiles. With laughter. As if it was a game I was supposed to play too.

The worst part? Everyone else seemed to play along. Even the teachers looked the other way.

They had this spot out by the field where they always sat Emma holding court in the middle, Tom and Ben flanking her like security. I used to walk the long way around just to avoid passing them.

Didn't matter. They noticed everything anyway.

"You always look like you're about to cry," Maya said to me once in the toilets. "It's kind of your thing, isn't it?"

Ben laughed from the stall. "Don't feel bad, Sarah. Some people peak in primary school."

They liked making people feel small. That was their power. And they used it like it was sport.

I remember bringing cupcakes in for a charity sale one Friday. I'd stayed up baking, even decorated them with tiny icing flowers. I thought maybe it would show them who I really was.

Ben took a bite, then spat it out, theatrically wiping his tongue.

"Are these poison?" he said, grinning at the others. "You trying to kill us, Sarah?"

Emma didn't even try to hide her laughter.

I stood there, frozen. Red in the face. Heart pounding.

No one said a word in my defence.

I started leaving early. Eating lunch in the library. Pretending to be sick when I couldn't face them. But they always found me—if not with words, then with looks. Whispers. Social media posts that weren't technically about me, but everyone knew they were.

It got so I couldn't trust anyone.

Every smile felt loaded. Every silence felt like judgment.

And the worst part? I started believing them. Started thinking maybe I was weird. Maybe I did bring it on myself.

But deep down, I knew the truth.

They were never kind. They were never my friends.

They were just better at pretending than I was.

And everyone let them.

It didn't stop. It got worse. Every week, something new chipped away at me, like they were slowly peeling back pieces of who I was and tossing them aside. First, it was my bag gone from the art room one afternoon and found hours later, drenched in toilet water, my sketchbook ruined. No one confessed, and no one helped. Then came the graffiti, scrawled in red marker across my final piece: try harder. It felt like a punch. That drawing had taken me weeks. I stared at the ruined paper while they laughed behind me, and no one not even my teacher said a word.

An anonymous Instagram account popped up a few days later. It followed only people at school. And it only posted one kind of thing photos of me. Old selfies I'd posted, pictures I didn't even know people had taken. One showed me sitting alone in the canteen, a caption underneath that read: loser vibes. Another: someone get her a mirror.

They started calling me "ghost girl" in the corridors. Not to my face, not exactly just loud enough so I'd hear. It was always followed by stifled laughter. I tried to ignore it, tried to walk faster, keep my head down. But the fear clung to me like a second skin. I couldn't eat in the canteen anymore. I stopped taking the bus. I even stopped talking in class, afraid that my voice even that would give them more ammunition.

The worst part? I started to believe what they said. That I was pathetic. That I was weird. That maybe I deserved it.

And still, no one stopped them.

*

Present Day

By the time dawn crept in through the curtains, none of us had moved. We stayed there, in Tom's living room, too wired to sleep, too scared to go home. Maya sat curled up in the armchair. Jamie paced. I stayed on the floor, back against the wall, staring at nothing.

We were waiting for a miracle. Or a call. Or a body.

Anything.

But the phone never rang.

No news.

No leads.

Tom was just… gone.

And we all knew how this story started. We'd lived it once already.

And the killer whoever they were wasn't done.

Because if we believed what the notes were saying, if we dared to read between the lines, there wa a message forming in the chaos. A pattern.

Each of us was part of something we hadn't truly understood when it happened. Something we had buried deep, hoping it would fade. Hoping no one would dig it back up.

But the past never stays buried. And now? It was clawing its way to the surface.

*

I looked out the window as the sun rose, casting the street in a soft, golden light that felt almost cruel. The world was still turning. People would be getting ready for work. Kids would be packing schoolbags. Cars would start pulling out of driveways.

And Tom was still missing.

I took my phone from my pocket and looked through the anonymous notes again. The ones I'd hidden in my drawer. The ones I almost didn't show anyone.

You pretend you're innocent.

But you know what you did.

One by one.

And now, this new one: *You left her there.*

It wasn't just about guilt anymore.

It was a countdown.

Whoever was behind this wasn't just trying to scare us.

They were planning something.

And if we didn't figure out who it was, and why, we were going to lose more people.

Maybe all of us.

*

I looked at Maya and Ben, the three of us bound together by something darker than friendship now. Bound by something unspoken.

And I realised we couldn't wait for the police to find answers.

We had to find them ourselves.

Before we were next.

17

DI Tee and DC Zak

The incident room felt different now.

The quiet hum of monitors, the shuffle of papers, the low murmur of officers, it all sat under a growing weight. The disappearance of Tom Weller hadn't just escalated the investigation; it had shifted it. The whiteboard had become a battlefield of red string and pinpoints, faces staring out like ghosts.

DI Tee stood with her arms folded, brow furrowed. The smell of stale coffee and whiteboard marker hung in the air. The board was a mess, but she could feel the pattern beneath it. Like a pulse, just under the skin.

"Tom didn't just vanish," she said quietly. "He was taken. Just like Sarah was silenced. This... this is planned."

DC Zak stood beside her, flipping through a file, eyes scanning a witness statement from Tom's mother.

"He texted a friend that night," Zak said. "Said he thought someone was following him. He never made it home."

Tee nodded grimly. "We're not dealing with random violence. This is personal. Directed."

She stepped closer to the board and pointed at the names — Sarah. Tom. Emma. Maya. Lily Barnes. Ben.

"Sarah and Tom. Victims. The others…?" She trailed off.

Zak finished the thought. "Connected. Same sixth form. Same friend group, more or less. But the details get darker the more you dig."

He handed her a slim folder, a copy of the school's safeguarding report from the year before. "Sarah was known to be quiet. Kept to herself. But there were multiple reports, mostly anonymous, that she was being harassed. Bullied. Subtle, persistent, damaging."

Tee scanned the notes. "No disciplinary action taken."

"No. Everything got buried under bureaucracy. Teachers 'monitored the situation' but did nothing."

She looked up, sharp. "What about Tom?"

Zak flipped to a separate sheet. "No reports. Tom was popular, teachers liked him, never had any issues."

Tee narrowed her eyes. "This isn't a game to them. It's a mission."

"Retribution," Zak said.

Tee let the word hang there.

Retribution.

It rang too true.

She turned back to the board. "We're missing the beginning. Something started all this. Not just the bullying. Something deeper. A trigger. We need to go back further. School records. Attendance. Staff notes. Friendships, breakups, fights, anything that fractured this group."

Zak nodded. "Want me to start with interviews again?"

"Yes. Start with the group. One-on-one. No shared narratives. See if their stories line up and more importantly, where they don't."

She paused, then added, "Start with Emma. She's already come forward once. There's guilt there. I want to know why."

*

Interview Room 2 – 10:41 a.m.

Emma sat with her arms wrapped tightly around herself, her usually polished appearance undone, hoodie sleeves tugged over her fingers, her once-perfect ponytail lopsided.

DC Zak entered quietly, offering a polite nod.

"Emma, thanks for coming in again. Can I get you anything?"
She shook her head, eyes downcast. "I just want this to stop."

He sat across from her, clipboard resting on the table between them. "We want that too. But we need the truth. All of it."

Emma swallowed hard. "I told you about the notes. I showed you everything."

"We know," Zak said gently. "And it helped. But this time… I want to talk about Sarah."

Her eyes flicked up sharply. Defensive. "What about her?"

"What was she like? At school."

Emma hesitated. "Quiet. Weird, I guess. She didn't talk to people much. She only came to our school for one lesson"

"Did people talk about her?"

Another pause. "Sometimes."

"Did they talk to her?"

Emma frowned. "Not really."

Ryan leaned in slightly. "Emma, were you one of the people who bullied her?"

Her silence was its own confession.

After a moment, she said, "We didn't mean to hurt her."

"But you did."

"She wasn't like us. She didn't get the jokes. She always looked scared. Like she thought everyone hated her."

Zak stayed quiet, letting the words fill the silence.

"She started crying once," Emma continued, her voice barely audible. "We were... we were laughing about something Ben said. I don't even remember what. But she just... broke. And we acted like it wasn't our fault."

"Why?"

"Because if we admitted it, then we'd have to feel bad. And we didn't want to. So we blamed her for being sensitive. Said she was overreacting."

Zak made a few notes. "And Tom?"

Emma's mouth twisted slightly. "Tom was different. He could be cruel, when we all joked he would always take it too far"

"Did you target Sarah?"

Emma shook her head. "No, she came to us. We just made her feel... less."

She looked up, eyes rimmed with tears.

"Do you think someone's coming for us?" she asked. "Because of what we did?"

Zak didn't answer. He just closed the folder.

*

Back in the incident room, Tee was waiting.

Zak gave her the debrief in low tones.

"She's not innocent. None of them are. And she knows it."

Tee nodded. "It was about power. They held it, Sarah didn't. Seems as though Tom was a driving force. Now someone's trying to tip the scales. But why hurt Sarah if she was a victim? Something isn't adding up. "

She turned back to the whiteboard. Her gaze settled on one of the few names that hadn't been crossed out: Ben

"Let's see what Ben has to say."

*

Interview Room 1 – 2:30 p.m.

Ben was nervous.

Shy. Defensive. Wearing battered old converse and fiddling with the tatty corners of the paperback book he carried.
He lounged in the chair, picking at the skin on his thumb every now and then, legs shaking.

"I'm not here to play games," Tee said as she took a seat. "Tom's missing. Sarah's dead. You need to tell me everything you know."

Ben looked at her, expression shifting.
"I didn't kill anyone."

"Didn't say you did."

She placed two photographs in front of him, Sarah, smiling faintly in her school portrait. And Tom, grinning beside a football trophy.

"Tell me about them."

Ben shifted. "Tom is my best friend, known him forever. Sarah was weird, I didn't really speak to her or know her well. She only came to our school for one lesson."

"You ever say anything to Sarah?"
He shrugged. "Maybe. Everyone did."

"You ever laugh when she cried?"

His jaw tightened.

"You ever call her names? Trash her sketchbook? Ruin her work?"

"I didn't touch her stuff."
"But you laughed when others did."

More silence.

Tee stared at him. "Someone is holding a mirror up to all of you. And you don't like what you see."

He looked up, sadness flaring in his eyes. "Why are you acting like it's our fault? We were just joking, we're young, it's banter."

"Banter?"

She leaned forward, voice low.
"If Tom ends up dead too… will you still say it was just banter?"

Ben had no answer.

Interview Room 3 – 3:45 p.m.

Maya had arrived late. She made a point of checking her phone right up until the moment she stepped into the interview room, rolling her eyes like she had better things to do. Designer jacket, flawless makeup, and the faint aroma of expensive perfume, she was composed, confident, and utterly unimpressed.

DC Zak sat across from her, his tone calm but firm.

"Thanks for coming in, Maya. I'm DC Zak and I just have a few questions to ask you today. Is that okay?"

She crossed her arms. "Didn't think I had a choice."

"Tom's missing. Sarah was found dead. These are serious events."

"I know," Maya replied, her voice flat. "But I don't know what you expect me to say. I wasn't involved."

Zak opened his file, careful to keep his expression neutral. "You were friends with both of them, correct?"

"Friends?" she laughed, though it came out as more of a scoff. "Tom, yeah. Sarah? No. I never even spoke to her."

He looked up. "Not once?"

"No," Maya said, now annoyed. "She was weird. Always hanging around by herself with her little sketchbook. I had no reason to talk to her."

"What about the times she was reported crying after class? Did you witness anything?"

"Look," Maya said, leaning forward. "You're asking the wrong person. If she cried, it was probably because she was unstable. People like that just… crack. It doesn't mean anyone did anything."

Zak paused. "Several students said she was bullied."

"By who?" Maya snapped. "Because it wasn't me. People love to throw around words like 'bullying' now. You so much as say someone's outfit is ugly and you're suddenly a monster."

"You ever say anything to her? About her clothes? Her art?"

Maya laughed again, this time colder. "I didn't even know she *did* art. And honestly, I didn't care."

Zak jotted something down. "Do you remember her first week at St Cedars?"

"No one forced her to be a loner," Maya said. "That was her choice."

Zak looked up. "You're very sure of that."

Maya shifted in her chair, defensive. "What are you trying to say? That I made her kill herself or something? Because that's ridiculous. I didn't even know her!"

"Kill herself? Maya, you know Sarah was murdered"

Maya shifted in her seat, as if she had said too much, "What difference does it make."

Zak closed the file gently. "You're not helping your case, Maya."

"What case?" Her voice rose. "I haven't done anything! I haven't hurt anyone."

"But you stood by. That's what we're trying to understand."

Maya's eyes flashed. "This is a waste of time."

She stood abruptly and stormed out without waiting to be dismissed.

Zak remained seated, the silence that followed her exit louder than her footsteps. After a moment, he whispered to himself:

"She's lying."

*

6 Months Earlier
Sarah

I knew something was off the second I got the message.

Come to the quarry tonight x — Emma.

She never messaged me. Not like that. Not with that kind of warmth, that kind of familiarity. We were never friends, not really — but sometimes she smiled at me in the halls, and that was enough to make me think maybe, just maybe, I belonged.

I told myself this could be the start of something. That maybe they'd finally seen me. Really seen me.

It was nearly dark when I got there. The air smelled like wet stone and smoke the fire they'd lit crackled lazily in the pit, shadows flickering against the jagged walls.

Emma stood near the edge, her arms folded, expression unreadable. Tom and Ben were there too, lounging on an old blanket, passing a bottle between them. They didn't look surprised to see me. Didn't smile.

And then Maya stepped out from behind the rocks.

That's when I knew.

"Hey," I said, cautious, already regretting every step I'd taken to get there. "You said to come."

Emma didn't answer.

Maya did. "We just thought it was time we had a little chat."

The word twisted in her mouth like a blade.

I barely had time to brace before she stepped forward and shoved me   hard. I stumbled back, the ground uneven beneath my feet. Laughter bubbled from behind her Ben's unmistakable snort, Tom's lazy chuckle.

I looked at Emma. Pleaded with my eyes. But she just stood there, hands limp at her sides, mouth a tight line.

"I didn't do anything," I said, trying to keep my voice steady. "I haven't even spoken to you"

"Exactly," Maya snapped, stepping closer. Her eyes burned. "You act like you're better than us. Quiet little Sarah with her books and her sad eyes. It's pathetic."

Then her fist connected with my stomach.

The pain stole the breath from me. I doubled over, gasping. Another blow this time to my ribs. My knees hit the dirt.

"Stop," I rasped, but no one moved.

Emma looked like she might cry. But she didn't move. She didn't stop it.

Maya grabbed a handful of my hair, yanked my face up to hers. "You say one word about this to anyone," she whispered, her voice ice-cold, "and I swear to God, I'll kill you. You hear me?"

I nodded. I couldn't do anything else.

She let go. I collapsed to the ground. Gravel cut into my skin, but I didn't feel it. Everything else hurt too much.

And just like that, they turned and left.
Their silhouettes vanished into the trees, laughter trailing behind them like smoke.

I lay there for a long time after, the stars above me cold and indifferent.

*

Later that evening, Tee sat in her office, the evidence board darkened by the falling dusk. Outside, the rain tapped gently against the windows.

Zak entered with a file in hand. "Preliminary forensics on the latest note, same paper stock as the others. Same ink, same pressure patterns. The killer's consistent."

He handed her another sheet. "But this is what matters, CCTV footage from outside Tom's house, roughly an hour before he went missing. No footage of Tom, but we caught a hooded figure slipping something into his letterbox."

Tee scanned the stills. Grainy, but clear enough to show intent.

Zak continued, "They've been watching them. Studying. Planning."

Tee nodded slowly. "This isn't a rampage. It's a ritual."

She turned toward the board one final time, gazing at the names, the faces, the notes.

Sarah.

Tom.
Emma.

Ben.

Maya.

Lily.

One by one.

*

Tee and Zak were knee-deep in the latest round of interview transcripts, the low hum of the fan in the corner doing little to cut through the thick tension in the incident room. Notes were scattered across the table, observations, contradictions, psychological profiles that didn't quite fit. Tee had just made a comment about the repetitive language used by Daniel in his last session, something about detachment and clinical distance, when Zak's phone buzzed sharply against the desk. He glanced at the screen, expecting another update from forensics, but his expression changed the second he answered. His eyes met Tee's across the cluttered desk, and he mouthed, "Another one." But as the voice on the other end continued, Zak sat up straighter, his grip tightening around the phone. "Multiple," he said aloud, the word cutting through the room like ice.

"This time, it's not just one." Tee was already grabbing her coat. Minutes later, they were in the car, the air thick with anticipation. The address took them to the edge of town, a quiet cul-de-sac backing onto the woods. Officers were already there, tape fluttering in the breeze, residents clustered behind hedges with phones in hand, hushed voices carrying like wind through leaves. The scene was worse than before. Three cats, maybe four it was hard to tell, the bodies arranged in a grim, deliberate display. Not just killed, but posed. Like someone had taken their time. Tee crouched, her jaw tight, eyes scanning the layout. Zak didn't speak at first, just exhaled slowly, the reality setting in. This wasn't escalation it was a declaration. Whoever was doing this had crossed a threshold. The cat killer wasn't fading away. They were just getting started.

The crime scene was a quiet patch of overgrown woodland just beyond the neat row of houses, where the trimmed lawns abruptly gave way to tangled underbrush and broken branches. It was the kind of place kids might use as a shortcut or teenagers might hang out on summer nights forgotten, tucked just out of sight. But nothing about it felt innocent now. The clearing was unnaturally still, choked with the scent of copper and damp earth. In the centre, the cats were arranged in a near-perfect semicircle, their bodies unnervingly precise, as if someone had placed them like props in a ritual. Each one bore signs of the same meticulous violence: no mess, no signs of panic, just clean, deliberate wounds. Their eyes had been closed, not naturally, but by force, lids pressed shut as though the killer couldn't bear to let them see. Around the clearing, police lights flashed red and blue against the trees, casting long, twitching shadows that made everything feel even more unreal. DC Zak stood just at the edge, staring at the arrangement with a sick feeling rising in his chest. DI Tee knelt beside the nearest body, her face unreadable, but her jaw clenched tight.

Zak crouched near the outer edge of the scene, his notebook half-forgotten in one hand. He'd seen every cat case since the first one six months ago, the ones that began as whispers on the neighbourhood forums, escalating into something more sinister, more calculated. But as he scanned the semi-circle of bodies laid out before him now, a quiet unease began to crawl beneath his skin.

"These aren't the same," he said aloud, though more to himself than anyone else.

Tee glanced over from where she was photographing the carved tree. "What do you mean?"

Zak rose slowly to his feet, brushing soil from his trousers. "The positioning. The earlier ones were messier. One or two cats at a time. Left in bins, alleys, doorsteps. Intimate places. Always isolated. Always private."

He gestured toward the deliberate arc of small, broken bodies, their limbs tucked like sleeping children.

"This this is a performance. Public. Symbolic. It feels staged for discovery. The others were impulsive, angry. This? This is… methodical."

He paused, eyes narrowing. "It's like a completely different signature."

Tee stood beside him now, silent. Zak could feel the weight of her attention shift not dismissing him, but analysing, recalibrating.

"Could be a copycat," she muttered. "Or an escalation."

"Maybe," Zak said, though he didn't sound convinced. "But the spacing, the incision points… These weren't done in a hurry. And the bodies they've been washed. Cleaned. That's new. Whoever did this, they weren't just angry. They were… in control."

Zak felt a chill trace his spine. Something about this scene wasn't just different it was wrong. As if they'd been chasing the wrong pattern all along.

"We've been looking for one killer," he said. "But what if there are two?"

Tee didn't answer. But the way she looked back at the cats told him she was already asking herself the same thing.

18

They thought no one saw.

They thought they were clever, cruel with a smile, venom dressed up as charisma. But I was there. I watched. Every. Single. Time.

Sarah never saw me.

She didn't know there was someone else in that building who watched her struggle to breathe while they smothered her with whispers and laughter.

She didn't see me behind the shelves in the art corridor, watching her tuck her ruined sketchbook under her arm and walk out with her head bowed.

She didn't hear the rage in my chest when Emma called her "fragile." When Maya fake-cried about Sarah's "vibes." When Ben mocked her drawings loud enough for the whole class to hear.

They called themselves a group, The Group, like they were some kind of royalty. St Cedars royalty. Unchallengeable. Untouchable.

But Sarah wasn't weak. That's the lie they told. That's the lie they needed to believe.

She was the strongest person I ever saw. Because she kept showing up. Day after day. She kept drawing. Kept breathing. Kept surviving them.

Until she didn't.

And when she was gone, when they realised they pushed too far, they cried crocodile tears and lit candles like they hadn't been dragging her into the dark for months.
That's when I made the decision, to set Sarah free.
One by one.

No mercy.

Because it wasn't just Sarah. I saw them torment others. Always the same formula: isolate, mock, humiliate. And always with that same performance of innocence.

Emma, the queen bee, always the orchestrator, always pretending to care. Ben, silent, calculated but complicit, the one who never said no, never stopped it. Maya venom in gloss. Lily, the echo chamber. Tom the joker who turned pain into punchlines.

But not anymore.

Now it's my turn to write the story.

And I don't need a sketchbook. I don't need canvas. Just fear.

And memory.

And blood.

*

Sometimes I see her in the mirror.

Her. Me. Both. Neither.

I look at my face, at the same features, the same hair, the same eyes, and I wonder who I really am anymore.

They tried to erase me. To make me invisible.

Now, I'll erase them.

Starting with Tom.

He ran, of course. They always run.

But I watched him all day. I knew his route home. I knew when he stopped to buy that Red Bull he always drank, like it could keep the guilt awake inside him.

I waited in the alley behind the derelict mechanics, a perfect pocket of shadow. He didn't even see me step out. Not until I whispered his name.

He turned. And in that second, that flash of recognition, he knew.

He knew who I was.

And he screamed.

I drove the needle in before he could run. A cocktail I'd made myself. Fast-acting. Not enough to kill. Just enough to paralyse. Just enough to give me time.

He collapsed, twitching, unable to cry out again. The fear in his eyes, real, raw, was more honest than anything that had ever come out of his mouth.

I dragged him to the basement I'd prepared. Just off the old train tracks. Soundproofed. Remote. Forgotten.

Stripped him of his pride. Of his mask.

I didn't torture him.
Not physically.

That would've been too easy.

Instead, I laid out photos. One by one. Photos of the damage he did, the hospital records.

And I made him look.

I made him see.

He tried to speak. Tried to lie. Even when he couldn't move, he still thought he could spin his way out. He whimpered something, I think it was "sorry." But it was too late for that.

So I took my time.

He was gone in under three minutes. Clean. Controlled.

He didn't bleed much. He just… stopped.

I left his body beneath the plastic sheeting, beneath the concrete I'd already cracked open in the far corner. I sealed it up again, neat, exact.

He won't be found for a while.

And by the time they do… it'll be too late.

I close the notebook, satisfied.

They thought they could forget.

They thought there'd be no consequences. They thought wrong.

Part Four

19

DI Tee and DC Zak

The shrill ring of the phone cut through the early morning quiet of the police station. DI Tee, her eyes still heavy with the exhaustion of the long night, reached out to grab the receiver, her fingers brushing against the cold plastic.

"DI Tee," she said, her voice steady despite the lingering fatigue.

The voice on the other end was urgent, but laced with a sense of discomfort. "Tee, it's Sergeant Jenkins. We've had a report come in from a concerned neighbour. Says there's a strange smell coming from an abandoned flat on the corner of Kingston Road. Doesn't sound like anything we'd usually handle, but the neighbours insistent. He says it's overpowering, something like rotting meat."

Tee's brow furrowed. She glanced at the clock, almost 3 a.m. The station was quiet, the only sound the soft tapping of keys on nearby desks. Another case, another mystery to solve. But this one felt different.

"Rotting meat?" Zak's voice drifted over from the adjacent desk. He was listening, his attention piqued.

"Yeah," Tee responded, her mind already racing. "Tom's still missing, shit. We need to go now".

She hung up the phone and turned to Zak, who was already pulling on his jacket. His eyes mirrored her unease.

"Let's go," he said.

Kingston Road — 3:03 a.m.

The cold, damp air of the early morning felt like it was crawling into their bones as Tee and Zak navigated through the narrow streets of Kingston Road. The buildings here were older, brick facades weathered by years of time, and the faint flicker of a few streetlights illuminated the wet pavement beneath their boots. The low hum of the city in the distance was muffled, and the quiet seemed almost oppressive, as though the entire town was holding its breath.

Tee's mind was still racing, the horrifying image of Tom sprawled lifeless playing on a loop in her mind. Could they be too late again? Had the killer already struck? The thought of it chilled her more than the night air.

Zak glanced at her, his eyes sharp, the usual calm that came with experience tempered by a growing urgency. "What do you think we're going to find inside?"

Tee didn't answer immediately. Her gaze moved from one building to the next, scanning for any signs of movement. "We need to be ready for anything."

They approached the building where the neighbour had mentioned the smell. The narrow entrance was dimly lit, the bakery's neon "Open" sign flickering faintly in the distance, casting an eerie glow over the street. They passed a delivery van, parked haphazardly, its tires still slick from the rain. The tension between them thickened with every step.

Zak's phone buzzed in his pocket. He pulled it out, his face hardening as he read the message. "Patrol's on their way. They'll be here in ten minutes."

Her pace quickened. "Let's move."

They ascended the narrow staircase at the back of the building, their footsteps echoing too loudly in the stillness of the night. When they reached the flat's door, Tee noticed it was slightly ajar, just enough for a draft to slip through, disturbing the musty air inside. She motioned for Zak to stay back, her hand reaching for her gun as she gently pushed the door open with her foot.

The flat was quiet. Too quiet.

Inside, everything appeared still. The low hum of an electronic device broke the silence, the screen of a paused video game flickering against the otherwise dim light.

Empty bottles of energy drinks, a pile of discarded pizza boxes, and clothes thrown carelessly across the furniture told the story of someone's disordered life.

Tee's eyes quickly scanned the room, but there was no sign of a struggle. No sign of forced entry. She stepped cautiously inside, her hand still on the grip of her weapon, a sense of foreboding settling over her.

Zak, still standing at the threshold, seemed to take a long breath and then gagged, "God that smell."

Tee nodded covering her nose with her arm, stepping further into the room, scanning for any clue that might have been missed in the dark. There was no visible sign of anything.

"Check the bedroom," Tee said, her voice quiet, but with an edge of command. "I'll check the bathroom and kitchen."

They moved quickly, splitting up to cover more ground. The hallway was as still as the living room, each door they passed slightly ajar, but nothing seemed out of the ordinary. The bathroom was empty, its lights flickering weakly above, the sink cluttered with toothpaste and soap. A typical bachelor's flat, almost too neat in its disarray.

Zak entered the bedroom, it was clear until he saw something strange. A door in the far corner that looked like it led downstairs, to a basement.

"Tee, you have got to come and see this." He called.

Tee made her way into the bedroom.
"Well the rest of the flat is clear, so." She hesitated when she could see what Zak was looking at.

"A basement in a downstairs flat." She whispered.

Tee and Zak made their way down the narrow steps into the basement, the air growing colder and heavier with each step. The door creaked shut behind them, sealing in the stench that had led them here—thick, putrid, and unmistakably the smell of decomposition. The basement was cloaked in shadows, their torches casting narrow beams of light across cracked concrete walls and rusted pipes. At first glance, it looked like any other abandoned storage space empty, damp, and long forgotten. But the smell told a different story.

They moved cautiously, scanning every corner. Tee paced toward the far end, where the scent was strongest. Her boot caught on something uneven—what looked like a lump of raised concrete near the corner of the room. She stumbled, catching herself against the wall with a muttered curse. Frustrated, she kicked at the obstruction. The piece of concrete shifted slightly, then cracked with a brittle snap as a chunk broke away. A foul gust of air escaped from the gap, and the torchlight revealed a hollow space beneath.

Zak stepped in quickly, shining his torch into the hole. What they saw made both of them recoil. A body twisted, pale, and half-covered in dirt. The unmistakable face of Tom stared blankly up at them, his features frozen in death, buried just beneath the surface of the basement floor.

Tom's body was crumpled into the gap, his eyes wide open and unblinking, his mouth slightly agape as if frozen in surprise. The unsettling thing was how serene his expression appeared, almost as if he were still in a deep sleep. But the pale colour of his skin and the faint bluish tint around his lips told a far more chilling story.

Zak checked for a pulse. Nothing. He pulled away and stood there for a moment, his hand tightening into a fist.

"Tom's dead," he said softly, not a trace of emotion in his voice, as if he was already preparing himself for the next step in their investigation. "Looks like the killer got to him first."

Tee walked forward, her eyes scanning the room. The body was too neat, no sign of a violent struggle, no blood splatter to indicate a frantic attack. The only clue that something was off was the faint metallic scent in the air.

"Poison," she said, her voice low. She could tell immediately. "Maybe pills. Maybe something stronger."

Zak raised his head from where he was kneeling beside the bed, his face grim. "So it's not just physical violence anymore. This is personal."

Tee's gaze lingered on Tom's motionless body. "They're playing a long game. But this isn't just about revenge. This is about control. It's methodical. Calculated. And we're still too far behind."

She straightened, brushing her hands off as though to shake off the chill creeping up her spine. The room had an unsettling quality now, something beyond the usual crime scene. The air seemed heavier, thicker. She could feel it pressing down on her.

There were no signs of forced entry, no broken locks, no forced windows. It looked as if Tom had let his killer in willingly. He had no idea what was coming, no clue that the person watching him online had been stalking him for days.

"Something doesn't add up," Zak murmured. "They couldn't have just lured him here."

Helen's eyes darted back to the open door. It was ajar just slightly, just enough to make it seem like he'd been caught off guard. She stepped out of the bedroom, scanning the rest of the flat again, looking for signs of where the killer might have been hiding, but there was nothing.

Zak stood next to her now, his face pale. "You think they're watching us now?"

Tee's gaze flicked back to Tom's lifeless form, then slowly turned toward the window. She could almost feel the weight of eyes on her, even though there was no one in sight.

"They're playing us, Zak. They're always been one step ahead. And now we've walked right into their trap. They clearly want to get caught but they're having a laugh, toying with us first."

The tension in the air grew even more suffocating as they both moved to the window, peering out onto the quiet street. The wet asphalt glistened under the streetlights, but there was no movement, no sign of anyone watching them.

Back at the Station — 6:00 a.m.

As the sun began to rise, the room at the police station felt like a tomb. The team had grown more tired, more fragmented. And now, the news of Tom's death had set everything into motion—but not in the way they'd hoped.

226

Zak, the quiet but meticulous DC who had been poring over old school records for days, had finally found something buried deeper than expected.

"Look at this," Zak said, pushing his laptop toward Tee. "I found something in Sarah's school logs. Took me hours to get access to the archived student files, but it was worth it."

Tee approached his desk, rubbing her eyes as she scanned the screen. "What am I looking at?"

Zak clicked into a file. "I was trying to track down Sarah's behavioural reports, see if there was any mention of who she was close with, or if there were early signs of distress. That's when I found the logs from her school counsellor. She'd been seeing someone regularly during the final term before her death."

Tee's brow furrowed. "Okay. That's not unusual, given what we know."

Zak gave a nod but didn't look up. "That's not all. I cross-referenced the appointment logs and, guess who else was seeing the same counsellor?"

Tee's breath caught. "Lily Shaw."

"What does the counsellor have to do with anything?" Tee asked

Zak looked up, locking eyes with both of them. "It's not about the counsellor, it's about what they were being treated for. They were both hospitalised after an overdose. They tried to take their own lives last year, right before all this started. But get this: the counsellor who was treating them at the time has a report in the files here. It's a crucial one."

Tee's heart skipped a beat. "Hospitalised?"

Zak nodded. "For a serious suicide attempt. And it wasn't the first time she had been in that state. The counsellor's notes show that Lily and Sarah had been in therapy for months, struggling to deal with what was happening at school."

Tee's eyes narrowed. "So they were already in crisis when all of this started?"

Zak confirmed. "Yes. And the most disturbing part according to the counsellor was that the bullying didn't stop there. Lily wasn't just a victim. She was part of the group that was bullying others, including Sarah. But not in the way you might think."

Tee's head swam with this new information. "What do you mean?"

Zak hesitated before continuing. "The counsellor mentions in their report that Lily was often bullied by the same group she was a part of. Emma her twin sister was at the heart of it."

"Emma?" Tee's voice was low with disbelief. "She's been bullying Lily too?"

Zak nodded grimly. "That's what it looks like. The report indicates that Lily tried to distance herself from the group but felt trapped. Emma was the ringleader, but she kept pushing Lily back into it. The notes show that Lily was conflicted she hated what was happening, but she didn't know how to stop it."

Tee ran her fingers through her hair. "So, Emma isn't just a victim she was actively participating in this?"

Zak clicked through the documents, pulling up an old entry in the school counsellor's notes.

"Here it is," Zak said, his voice quiet. "According to the notes, Emma played a major role in ostracising Lily from the rest of the group. She encouraged the others to ignore Lily, to isolate her. And that wasn't even the worst of it. She actively ridiculed Lily's emotional struggles, calling her 'weak' and 'dramatic' in front of the others. It's no wonder Lily was so lost."

Tee's mind raced. She could feel the pieces shifting together, falling into place with sickening precision. "This is bigger than we thought. Emma wasn't a bystander in this. She was the instigator."

Zak looked as though the gravity of it was just hitting him. "And now Lily, the twin we never really thought about, has been living in her shadow. This... this could explain everything. All the rage."

"Zak you have really outdone yourself, nice work." Tee says whilst slapping him on the back.

"You wouldn't believe how many hoops I had to jump through, I had to charm that many people I was even starting to charm myself." said Zak with a smirk.

Tee rolled her eyes with a smile.

Zak looked up from the computer. "I'm going to speak with the counsellor. I think it's time we hear the full story, before we talk to Lily."

The Counsellor's Office — 9:00 a.m.

The office was small and cozy, the kind of space designed to make broken things feel safe. Soft lighting bathed the room in a golden glow, while the faint scent of lavender drifted from a plug-in diffuser near the door, subtle but constant like a quiet promise that this was a place where nothing bad could reach you, at least for a little while. The shelves sagged under the weight of well-thumbed self-help paperbacks and trauma recovery guides, spines faded, corners curled. A cluttered stack of laminated leaflets fanned across the side table bore titles like *"When Words Are Hard," "Supporting Adolescents Through Loss,"* and *"The Quiet Crisis: Teenage Grief and Guilt."*

A warm-toned floor lamp stood in the corner like a sentinel, casting a pool of gentle light across a faded rug and a pair of mismatched chairs both worn but clean, like everything else in the room. On her tidy desk sat a ceramic mug with a small chip on the handle, steam no longer rising, and a neatly polished brass plaque that read:

MS. S. MILLFIELD
Specialist Student Welfare & Support Services

She was in her late fifties, though she moved with the quiet weariness of someone who had carried too many stories on her back. Her greying hair curled softly around her ears in a loose bob, gently frizzed at the ends, and she wore her usual cardigan oatmeal-coloured and buttoned just once near the top over a faded floral blouse. The sleeves were pushed up past her elbows in quiet defiance of the room's chill, her forearms lightly freckled, the skin marked with years but unhidden. A thin, woven bracelet bright with green and red thread, clung to one wrist, slightly frayed, clearly handmade.

She didn't wear makeup. She didn't need to. Her presence was its own balm. She had the kind of voice that made you stop holding your breath without realising it. And her eyes soft but endlessly observant always seemed to be reading between the lines of what you said. She didn't smile much, but when she did, it wasn't forced. It was the kind of smile that made you feel seen.

She had become something of a quiet pillar in the borough's schools called in when things were unraveling, when other adults didn't know what to say anymore. She never made a show of knowing better, but she usually did. Calm. Effective. Discreet. The woman who held space for pain like it was something sacred. And the one who, if you let her, could take even your worst secret and somehow make you believe you weren't beyond saving.

Listening to the next generation of broken kids. When they come to her she had recognises the signs immediately not just of suffering, but of kinship. She takes on her cases personally. Took notes. Asked the right questions.

"Detectives, I wasn't expecting you this morning," She said, standing up. "Is there anything I can help with, were the notes all okay that I sent over?"

Tee closed the door behind her. "They were a really great help thank you, but we need to hear from your point of view, some crucial information about Lily Shaw and her twin, Emma."

The counsellor's eyes shifted with something between apprehension and resignation. "I see. You're asking about Lily Shaw."

Zak stepped forward. "We've been looking into the group of students she was involved with Emma, Tom, Maya and Ben, in particular. And we've come across disturbing information suggesting that Lily was bullied and hospitalised."

The counsellor's expression softened, as if she had been expecting this moment. She nodded slowly.

"Lily came to me many times. I remember her so clearly. But... her situation was complicated. She was torn between wanting to be accepted by the group and feeling utterly rejected by them. Emma was always at the heart of it. Always."

"Did you know that Emma was bullying her too?" Zak asked quietly.

The counsellor paused, headed over to her filing cabinet and took out a file. She started to flick through the pages until she found the right one. "It wasn't always obvious. But yes, Emma did play a part. According to Lily didn't do it outright, but she isolated Lily. When Lily was at her lowest, Emma would make jokes, sarcastic comments. She made her feel worthless in ways no one else could."

Tee clenched her fists, anger rising in her chest. "And no one did anything? Assuming the school knew... the staff... how could they let it go on like this?"

The counsellor looked ashamed. "The parents tried to intervene, but it wasn't enough. Emma was the golden child. She was popular, connected, and when Lily tried to speak up about her pain, she wasn't taken seriously. Emma knew how to manipulate the situation. And Lily... Lily was just too afraid to fight back."

The counsellor swallowed hard. "Lily never spoke about Emma much after the incident last year. She was afraid of her sister, in a way. Afraid of what would happen if she told the truth. But... I remember her mentioning something once. She said Emma was the one person who knew what it felt like to be invisible. And she said that was the hardest thing about it—being invisible even to her own twin."

Tee felt a shiver run through her. "And what did she mean by that?"

The counsellor's voice dropped to a whisper. "I don't know. But I do know one thing for sure Lily just wanted to be seen."

"What can you tell us about Sarah, similar story?" Zak asked.

Tee flipped through the file in front of her, eyes skimming over neatly typed notes, each line a quiet scream buried in professional language. Sarah had been seeing Ms. Millfield for over a year, the sessions beginning after multiple referrals from teachers concerned about her isolation and erratic attendance.

The notes detailed a consistent pattern: anxiety, social withdrawal, signs of trauma. But what stood out most were the final few entries, vague but troubling references to group pressure, manipulation, and a deepening sense of hopelessness. In one session, Sarah had apparently described "feeling hunted, even in silence," and hinted that someone knew everything about her, but the counsellor hadn't pushed for a name. "Sarah struggled with trust," Ms. Millfield explained softly, hands folded in her lap. "She carried her pain like a secret."

Her voice dropped lower, full of quiet grief. "I should've pushed. I keep asking myself that. What if I'd just asked her one more time?"

There was a long pause.

She folded her hands in her lap, composed but trembling slightly. "I want you to find whoever did this. I don't care how long it takes. She didn't deserve what happened. She was she was so gentle. And she was trying. She was trying so hard to stay afloat."

The detectives nodded.

Back at the Station — 12:30 p.m.

Tee and Zak sat in the bullpen, exhausted and defeated by the scene they'd just left behind. Their minds were whirling, trying to piece together the puzzle that seemed to grow more complex with each new victim.

"You might want to see this," Zak said, his voice quieter than usual.

Tee and Zak exchanged a glance before following him to the desk. Zak pulled up the CCTV footage of Tom's last known location. The timestamp matched Tom's social media post, he'd tagged the coffee shop just an hour before his death.

"There's something strange," Zak said, tapping the mouse to rewind the footage. "Look at the background."

235

On the grainy video, a shadow moved behind Tom as he sat at the table inside the coffee shop. A hooded figure, walking past just a flash, but unmistakable. Their features were hidden in the blur, but the shape, the silhouette…

"That's the same hoodie we saw following Sarah," Tee whispered.

Zak nodded. "They were watching him, so close by. We missed them in plain sight."

And just like that, the case took another turn.

20

The news broke early on a grey Thursday morning. Tom's body had been discovered in the basement of an abandoned building on Kingston Road. The official statement was brief: "Being treated as suspicious." In our small town, where everyone knew everyone, the implications were profound.

For weeks, Tom had been missing. His absence was a constant undercurrent in our daily lives, a void that grew more palpable with each passing day. Now, with the confirmation of his death, that void became a chasm, swallowing any hope we had clung to.

Maya, was the first to retreat into herself. Once vibrant and full of life, she became a shadow, her presence barely noticeable. She stopped coming out, her phone went unanswered, and her social media accounts fell silent. We tried to reach out, but she remained unreachable, ensnared in her grief.

I remembered the last time I saw her, sitting alone on a park bench, staring blankly ahead. I approached, but she didn't acknowledge me. Her eyes, once so expressive, were now vacant.

Desperate for connection, I turned to Lily. We had grown distant over the past year, but I hoped that shared grief might bridge the gap. I found her in the garden engrossed in a book.

"Lily," I began hesitantly, "have you heard about Tom?"

She looked up, her expression unreadable. "Yes."
"I can't believe he's gone. It's... it's devastating."

She closed her book slowly. "Is it?"

I was taken aback. "What do you mean?"

"Tom was cruel," she said flatly. "He tormented people, made their lives miserable. Maybe the world is better off without him."

Her words stung. "That's a horrible thing to say."

She shrugged. "Sometimes the truth is horrible."

Lily's reaction haunted me. I began to reflect on our past, the dynamics within our group. Tom had been charismatic, the life of the party, but there were moments subtle, often dismissed where his behaviour crossed lines. He had a knack for finding people's insecurities and exploiting them, all under the guise of humour.

I thought about Maya, how she often laughed off Tom's biting remarks, how she seemed to shrink in his presence. I thought about Lily, who had once been full of life but had gradually withdrawn, her spark dimmed.

Had we all been complicit? Had we enabled Tom's behaviour by staying silent?

*

Determined to make amends, I reached out to Lily again. This time, I found her in her room, painting.

"I'm sorry," I said. "For everything. For not seeing what was happening, for not standing up."

She looked at me, her eyes softening slightly. "It's not about apologies, Emma. It's about change."

"I want to change. I want to be better."

She nodded. "Then start by listening. Really listening."

*

In the weeks that followed, our group fractured. Some distanced themselves, unable to face the reality of our past. Others, like me, sought to understand, to grow.

Maya eventually started to come out again, quieter but still assertive. She joined a support group, sharing her experiences and helping others.

Lily and I rebuilt our friendship, slowly, with honesty and vulnerability. We acknowledged our mistakes, our complicity, and vowed to do better.

Tom's death was a tragedy, but it forced us to confront uncomfortable truths. It shattered the illusion of our perfect group and exposed the cracks we had long ignored. In the aftermath, we found a chance for redemption, for growth, and for genuine connection.

*

I found it by accident.

It was one of those grey, soulless afternoons, the kind that hovers in limbo between rain and silence. I'd gone into the garage to help Mum clear out some of the old boxes. She said she couldn't look at them anymore. Said they made the house feel heavier, as if Lily's shadows had settled into every corner since she came home from the hospital but never quite came back.

I didn't expect to find anything important. I was just doing my part, playing the helpful sister, the responsible daughter. The one who smiled at the neighbours and said she was "doing fine" when they asked. The one who hadn't completely broken everything.

But then one of the old cardboard boxes collapsed as I was moving it. Papers spilled everywhere scribbled schoolwork, doodles, abandoned diary entries. I picked them up one by one, not really seeing them, until something caught my eye: a thick folder with a cracked plastic cover, buried beneath a pile of yellowing worksheets.

It opened easily, too easily, and I wish it hadn't.

Inside were scraps of paper. No titles. No explanation. Just screenshots. Printed pages. Snippets of online chats and text threads. The kind of thing you'd only collect if you were trying to remember what people said or prove it.

At first, I didn't understand. I thought it was just old notes. Random screenshots from school. But then I saw my name.

My messages.

From me. From Maya. From Ben. From Tom.

Stupid things. Throwaway jokes. Comments we thought were funny. I remembered the moments — on the bus, in class, on the group chat we never gave a second thought to. But reading them now, with the words staring back at me in stark, black font on thin white paper, my stomach turned.

They weren't jokes.

"Why do you even hang around us?"

"You're so weird, Lily."

"Maybe if you smiled once in a while people would actually like you."

"Don't you own a hairbrush?"

Each message was like a pinprick to my skin, small but sharp, and together they formed a pattern — one I hadn't wanted to see. There were even screenshots of us laughing after she left group calls. Of Maya mocking the way she spoke. Of Tom calling her "a ghost with no personality." And me, I wasn't just there. I participated. I encouraged it. I called it banter. I thought we were being edgy, funny. That Lily was just too sensitive, that she should've grown a thicker skin.

But there it was, a curated scrapbook of cruelty.

And she'd kept it.

Tears blurred my vision before I even realised I was crying. My hands were shaking, and the folder slipped from my grip, pages fluttering to the dusty floor like discarded confessions.

And then I saw it. Tucked between two sheets was a hospital bracelet. Faded print. Crumpled edge. But still legible.

Lily Shaw
Admission Date: November 18th

I stared at the date for a long time.

The same week we told ourselves she was "just being dramatic."

I sank to the floor, pressing the bracelet to my chest like it could somehow undo the damage. I remembered how relieved we were when she stopped showing up. How we didn't have to watch what we said anymore. How Maya had even joked that we'd "edited the group down to the best bits."

And Lily... Lily had been alone. Completely, utterly alone.

We hadn't just ignored her.

We'd broken her.

Every cruel word, every exclusion, every whispered laugh when she tripped or said the wrong thing it was all right here, documented in painful detail. She had kept it. All of it. Like she knew she'd need to show someone someday. Like she knew no one would believe her otherwise.

I felt sick. A deep, gnawing sickness that started in my gut and climbed all the way to my throat. I wanted to scream. I wanted to go back and fix it. To tell her I was sorry. To beg for forgiveness.

But it was too late.

The damage was done.

*

I went to find her that night.

It was almost midnight. The house was quiet. Mum and Dad were asleep, their room down the hall like an island I couldn't reach. I stood outside Lily's door for a full minute, my hand hovering near the knob. We hadn't talked much since Tom's body was found. None of us had. The silence was deafening — an empty house full of unsaid things.

When I finally knocked, the door creaked open on its own. She was sitting on her bed, the light from her laptop casting shadows across her face. She didn't look up.

I swallowed. My mouth was dry. "Lily?"

Nothing.

I stepped in slowly. "I… I found some of your things in the garage."

That made her turn.

Her eyes were dark, unreadable. Not angry. Not even sad. Just… distant. Like someone watching the world from behind glass.

"You shouldn't go through my stuff," she said. Her voice was flat. Unbothered.

"I wasn't trying to," I said quickly. "It just… fell out. The folder."

Her eyes lingered on me. "Did you read it?"

I didn't lie. "Yes."

A pause. Then, "Good."

I flinched at the word. "Lily, I didn't know. I swear, I didn't realise how bad it was. I didn't think—"

"That's the problem," she said quietly. "None of you ever did."

I wanted to cry. I wanted to fall to my knees and tell her how sorry I was. But she didn't want that. Not from me. Not now.

"I just…" I tried again. "Tom's gone. And Maya she won't speak to anyone. Ben's losing it. We're all… falling apart."

She tilted her head. "And?"

Her voice was ice. I stared at her. "What do you mean, and?"

She looked back at the laptop screen. "Tom was cruel. They all were. Maya. Ben. You."

I opened my mouth, but no words came.

"I used to think it was me," she continued. "That there was something wrong with me. That if I tried harder, smiled more, spoke less, dressed differently maybe you'd let me stay."

My heart cracked with every word.

"But now?" She turned back to me, eyes narrowed. "Now I don't care what happens to any of you."

It hit like a slap.
"I'm your sister," I whispered.
She laughed a cold, hollow sound.

But Lily wasn't looking at me anymore.

The conversation was over.

I left her room in silence, the weight of her words dragging behind me like chains.

*

Over the next few days, the guilt dug deeper. Maya stopped responding to texts again and her parents said she wasn't up for visitors. Ben was spiralling, paranoid and snappy, jumping at shadows and accusing every one of knowing more than they said.

The fear was growing. Something was wrong.

Tom hadn't just died.

He'd been placed. Hidden. Buried. Left like a message.

And we were the intended readers.

But the scariest thing wasn't the possibility that someone out there was picking us off one by one.

The scariest thing was the idea that maybe Lily had known. Maybe she had watched it all happen, or worse, did it.

*

I stayed up late that night, pacing my room, rereading the texts from the folder in my head, wondering how I had been so blind. How we had all been.

Lily had warned us. In her silence. In her withdrawal. In the way she flinched when we laughed too loud.

And now the silence was turning into something else.

Something colder.

Sharper.

And I didn't know how to stop it.

Or if I even deserved to.

21

I remember the night she tried to leave this world.

The way the call came in urgent, panicked, barely coherent. The paramedics with their blank professionalism, moving around the scene with cold efficiency. The empty bottle on the floor. The silence that had soaked into the walls like blood.

I remember how small she looked.

How still.

Lily had always been quiet, always the observer, but that night God, that night she looked like she had disappeared. Like she'd finally succeeded in becoming invisible.

It was a blur. White lights. Chemical air. The beeping of machines that seemed far too loud and far too fragile. One small malfunction, and it would all stop.

They whispered it when they thought I couldn't hear. "Too much in her system." "No response." "We'll have to wait and see."

And something in *me* broke with it.

*

I remember the teachers.

The ones who said they had "no idea."

The headmaster with his sympathetic frown. The counsellor who "did all she could." The form tutor who sent home a card and a teddy bear like it was a scraped knee and not a suicide attempt.

They didn't know?

Bullshit.

I saw it every day. I watched her flinch when Emma made another jab. When Ben whispered about her behind his hand. When Tom sneered and told her she looked like a corpse. When Maya rolled her eyes and said, "Why is your sister even here?"

Every day, a thousand tiny knives. The kind that didn't leave marks you could photograph. No bruises. No evidence. Just a slow erosion.

Until there was nothing left.

And they laughed. They *laughed* while she died inside.

If she came back, if even a piece of her returned, I would make it right.

I would make them see what they did.

I would make them *feel* it.

And if she didn't?

Then I would become the part of her that they couldn't destroy.

*

People like to talk about breaking points.

Singular moments where everything snaps, and something darker takes over.

But for me, it wasn't a snap.

It was a slow, silent splitting.

Like a crack through ice that grows with every step until suddenly, you're falling through.
I didn't wake up one day and decide to become something else.

I *watched* it happen.

And in the space where she once existed, I became something colder. Something sharper. Something made entirely of the pieces they left behind.

I didn't scream.

I planned.

*

The first time was easy.

I followed Sarah at a distance, just watching. Just curious.
But then she turned down the alley near the old canal.

And something in me whispered: *Now.*

I didn't even think. Not really.

She turned. I moved. One simple move.

I stood there, breathing hard, heart pounding in my throat,
watching the ripples fade.

I thought I'd feel guilt.
But I felt… calm.

Like I had just taken my first real breath in months.

*

Tom was harder.

Not physically, he was too arrogant to ever think someone might come for him. But he was cruel in ways that lingered. He got into your head. Twisted things around. Made you doubt what was real.

I waited with him.

Talked to him.

Laughed.

And when the time came, I didn't hesitate.

The look on his face, that brief flicker of confusion, then fear, it should've haunted me.

But it didn't.

It felt like justice.

I'm not sorry for what I've done.

Let me say that again.

I'm not sorry.

Not for Sarah.

Not for Tom.

Not even for the fear in their little group now Emma, Maya, the others walking around like they might be next. Because they might be. They built the game. I'm just playing by their rules now.

They taught me how to smile while lying.

How to laugh while someone cries.

How to twist the knife and call it *banter.*

I learned from the best.

I watch them try to make sense of it all the whispers, the fear creeping in at the edges of their perfect lives. They look for someone to blame, someone to hold responsible, because the truth feels too slippery, too uncomfortable.

Emma's been quieter lately. There's something guarded in the way she moves, like she's only just realising how fragile everything really is. I see it in the way she glances at empty chairs. In the pauses between her sentences. She's not the same girl who laughed so easily.

I hear the questions they ask about Tom, about Sarah. I read between the lines in their voices. They're reaching for explanations, for something neat and digestible. Their undertone riddled with guilt, even though they still don't really see what toxic poison they are.

But life doesn't work like that. Pain doesn't always have a clean beginning, and guilt doesn't come with a name tag.

Sometimes the consequences just arrive. Quietly. Unstoppable.

And when they do, no one ever sees them coming.

*

Sometimes, late at night, I sit with Lily while she sleeps.

She doesn't know I do it. But I sit there and watch her breathing. I imagine what she'd say if she found out. If she saw what I've become.

Maybe she'd be horrified.

Maybe she'd cry.

Or maybe just maybe she'd understand.

Because I'm not doing this out of hate.
Not really.

*

I always said we were two of a kind.

Different face. Different laugh. Same sorrow.

But now?

Now we're not the same anymore.

She broke.

I didn't.

She drowned.

I swam.

And I'm going to drag every single one of them into the deep with me.

22

Emma

I didn't sleep again. Not really.

I lay in bed, tangled in the sheets like a spiderweb I couldn't escape from, staring up at the ceiling. The familiar creaks of the house settled into the silence like footsteps I wasn't sure were real. The radiator ticked in that annoying, irregular way it always did when the heat was shifting through the pipes. Somewhere down the road, a car passed, the low hum of its engine disappearing into the night.

Every time I closed my eyes, I saw Tom's face, first the way I remembered him, smiling, cocky, a little cruel in that way boys can be when they think no one's looking. Then I saw him as I imagined him now. Cold. Still. Crushed under layers of dirt and concrete. Not even a proper grave.

Dead.

Gone.

And every time I thought of him, I thought of Lily.

Lily, who had once clung to me like I was the only thing anchoring her to this world. Like I was air, and she couldn't breathe without me.

Lily, who now looked through me like I was already a ghost.

I turned over, pulled the duvet tighter, and tried to will myself to sleep. But sleep didn't come. It hadn't in days.

Not since the police came.

Not since they found Tom's body.

Not since the world cracked open at the seams and everything fell through.

*

The days felt like walking through smoke.

Everything blurred. Everyone moved like shadows. Faces were indistinct. Conversations floated around me but never touched me. It was like I was drifting through a dream, one of those slow, suffocating ones where you know you're not really awake but you can't claw your way out.

People stared.

That was the worst part. They stared, and no one said anything.

It was like they already knew the truth, some truth I hadn't even admitted to myself yet and they were just waiting for me to crack. Waiting for me to collapse under the weight of it and scream *I did it. I killed him. I deserve this.*

Except I hadn't.
Not really.

Right?

*

Maya hadn't spoken since the news about Tom broke. She came out, technically, but she wasn't *there*. Her body was just sat. Her name was marked present. But whatever part of her had once been Maya, bright, sarcastic, always whispering jokes at the worst possible time that part was gone.

I went for my usual walk and saw Maya sitting alone by the bandstand.

"Maya," I said, approaching her slowly, like she was a wild animal that might bolt or bite. "Can I sit?"
She didn't look up.

Didn't blink.

Didn't move.

I sat anyway, heart thudding like I was the one being hunted now.

"I'm—"

"You don't get to be sorry," she said quietly, her eyes still on the ground "Not anymore."

The way she said it made my skin crawl. Cold. Hollow. Final.

She stood and walked away.

*

I found Lily later.

She was sat in the garden by the summer house, her usual sketching place. She had her arms crossed, oversized blouse draped around her slender frame, the wind lifting the hem just enough to make her look weightless.

She was watching the sky like it had done something wrong.

I hesitated. Then I stepped closer.

"I miss you," I said.

The words felt stupid. Too small. But I had to say something.

"I know I don't have the right to say that," I added. "But I do."

She didn't turn.

Didn't flinch.

Just stood there, the wind catching her hair, her profile sharp against the grey sky.

"We were best friends," I said. "Before all of this. Before... before I turned into someone else."

Slowly, she turned to face me.

Her eyes were unreadable. Dark. Cold. Not angry something worse. Detached.

"You didn't turn into someone else," she said.

Her voice was calm, but every word landed like a slap.

"You just stopped pretending you weren't already that person."

261

I stepped back.

It felt like she'd punched me. Like something inside me broke, and I wasn't even sure what it was yet.

"That's not fair."

"No," she agreed. "It's not."

Then she tilted her head, studying me like I was a specimen. Like I was something she was trying to figure out whether to dissect or throw away.

"What wasn't fair," she said slowly, "was being laughed at every day. Being pushed to the edge. And then being told I was the problem. Feeling like I didn't deserve to walk the same earth or breathe the same air."

There it was again.

That edge in her voice.

That sharpness.

I swallowed, suddenly unsure of myself. "You think I deserved to lose them?"

She didn't blink.

"Again, you've somehow made it all about you. I think you should count yourself lucky you haven't lost more."

She rolled her eyes, and walked away.

And I just stood there, alone in the wind, feeling like I had lost everything.

*

That night, I went back to the garage.

Back to the old storage boxes and forgotten shelves. Back to the folder.

The one I'd found by accident the week after everything happened, the one Lily had kept hidden.

I hadn't opened it since.
Hadn't dared.
But something told me I had to.

That there was more.

I sat on the floor, legs crossed, the folder in my lap.

I opened it.

Inside: documents, timelines, printed messages.

She had documented everything.

Every insult. Every rumour. Every whisper behind her back.

Every time we pushed her aside. Every time we called her a freak. Every time we left her out on purpose, then told her she was being dramatic when she got upset.

Ben. Tom. Maya.
Me.

Even the teachers.

There were screenshots emails to staff, messages begging for help, time-stamped and marked "read" but never replied to.

One note stood out. Handwritten.

Two weeks before she took the pills.

"If this doesn't work, I have to become someone stronger. Someone they can't break."
My breath caught.
My hands shook.

This wasn't just a girl who got hurt.

This was a girl who'd been systematically dismantled.

And then rebuilt herself into something else.

Something colder.

Something terrifying.

*

The next day, I asked to speak to the counsellor, the same counsellor the school sends everyone too.

Her office was small. Cluttered. A diffuser puffed lavender-scented mist into the air like it could erase the things people confessed inside those walls.

She looked surprised to see me.

"Emma," she said, folding her hands. "I was surprised you reached out."

"I need to understand," I said. "About Lily. What happened to her."

Her expression shifted.

Careful.

"You know I can't disclose—"

"I know," I interrupted. "But please. I think someone might be in danger."
That got her attention.

She studied me for a long moment. Then nodded, just slightly.

"Lily came to see me," she said. "The year before it happened."
She paused. She hesitantly went to her filing cabinet to retrieve Lily's file.

"She was anxious. Isolated. She felt trapped by your shadow. But more than that, she felt... hunted."

I frowned. "Hunted?"

"She said it was like being circled by wolves. Your group, she felt targeted by you. Constantly scrutinised. Made into a joke."

My chest tightened.

"She said her twin, Emma was the worst of all."

It hit me like ice water.

"She said that?"

The counsellor nodded.

"That you would smile to her face, then laugh behind her back. That you once told her she should be grateful to have you."

My stomach turned.

I remembered that conversation. I hadn't meant it the way it sounded. Had I?

"She begged for help," the counsellor continued. "I referred her to outside services. Her parents said she was doing better. But I knew she wasn't."

"She tried to kill herself," I whispered.

"Yes," the counsellor said simply. "She did."

There was a long pause.

"She survived," I said.

The counsellor nodded.

"But something inside her didn't."

*

I sat outside the office for almost an hour.

Just breathing.

Trying to process.

Trying to piece together all the versions of Lily that had existed.

The one who used to braid my hair and sleep over on weekends.

The one who had cried when Tom laughed at her presentation.
The one who had taken a bottle of pills and left behind a note that read like a manifesto.

She hadn't just broken.

She had changed.

Morphed.

Transformed.

Into what, I wasn't sure.

But it wasn't the Lily I had known.

Not anymore.

*

Back home, I sat on my bed and reread the note from the folder.

"Someone they can't break."

That wasn't a cry for help.

That was a declaration.

She hadn't come back weaker.
She had come back with a plan.

Ben was gone, he didn't want anything to do with us.

Tom was dead.

Maya was unraveling.

And me?

I was next.

Because if someone was behind all of this, if someone had orchestrated the ruin of our little kingdom, then I had a feeling I knew exactly who it was.

And she wore my face.

Before

Lily had always known there was something a little off about being the other twin.

People liked Emma. They smiled at her in hallways. Teachers praised her in front of the class. Boys turned their heads when she laughed too loud.

Lily just existed in Emma's shadow.

Still, there had been a time—brief, fragile—when she was part of the group. Included in the way you include a stray cat who won't stop hanging around: tolerated. Fed scraps.

But it changed. Slowly at first. Then all at once.

*

It started with whispers.

"Lily looks like she cut her own hair with garden shears."

"Do you think she knows leggings aren't pants?"

"She always smells like anxiety and budget shampoo."

Sometimes she heard them. Sometimes they wanted her to. Emma always laughed the loudest.

Lily tried to fit in. She dressed like them, talked like them, copied Emma's eyeliner even though it made her eyes sting. But it never worked. There was always something wrong.

Like the day they all wore chokers to school—just a dumb trend. Lily showed up wearing one too.

Emma looked her up and down in front of everyone and said, "You look like you're trying to cosplay someone with a personality."

The group howled.

Even Maya laughed.

Lily pulled the choker off in the girls' bathroom and threw it away.

She didn't cry.

Not then.

Then came the messages.

A group chat—The Inner Circle.

Lily had been part of it once.

Until she wasn't.

They made a new chat and forgot to remove her from the old one.

She read everything.

"She's like a glitch in the simulation. Even her laugh is off."

"Emma, you've got to fix your twin."

"Maybe she's adopted?"

"No one would choose that."

Emma had typed that last one. Lily stared at it for hours. No one deleted it. No one apologised.

Ben started calling her Static.

Because "she buzzes around and gives everyone a headache."

Maya told her she needed "serious fashion therapy."

Said it like it was a joke.

Said it in front of people.

One day, someone printed out a fake flyer for a "How Not to Be Weird" seminar and taped it to her locker.

Under "Presenter," it read: Literally Anyone But Lily.

She didn't even tear it down. She just walked away.

But it was Tom who broke her. It was Tom who left her shaking.

The hallway was quiet after school. That strange kind of silence where every sound echoes too loud. Lockers loomed like sentries. Lily bent to pick up her books—she'd dropped them again, hands clumsy, nerves frayed from a day full of sidelong glances and quiet snickers.

Tom was leaning against the lockers.
He didn't move to help.
He just watched.

She tried not to look at him, but her eyes flicked up. Just once.

Mistake.

He smirked.

"Still trying?" he said.

273

She blinked. "What?"

"To be one of us."

She stiffened. Said nothing.

He stepped closer. His voice lowered, soft and almost sympathetic. That made it worse.

"You really don't get it, do you?"

Her throat closed up.

"You were never part of it. You were the warm-up act. The entertainment. A punchline dressed up in your sister's clothes."

He crouched, so his face was level with hers. She could see the flecks of gold in his eyes.
He looked straight at her and didn't blink.
"You're not Emma. You'll never be Emma. And the only reason anyone tolerated you was because she asked us to. Because she felt bad."

He tilted his head, studying her like a dead bird on the pavement.
"But even she gave up eventually."

Lily's fingers curled into the cover of her notebook.

Tom leaned in a little closer.
"And between you and me?" he whispered. "There's something wrong with you."

Her breath caught.

"You creep people out. You ruin rooms just by walking into them. Everyone feels it. The teachers. The guys. Even your own sister. You're like this… hole. Like you suck the air out of everything. You don't belong. Anywhere."

He stood slowly.

"I mean, look at you," he said, almost bored now. "You're like a glitch in the system. Like someone tried to copy Emma, but the file got corrupted."
He let that hang in the air.
And then, over his shoulder as he walked away:
"Honestly, if you disappeared tomorrow, no one would even notice. Or care. Least of all her."

Lily didn't move.

Couldn't move.

She stayed there on the floor for a long time, knees drawn up, arms wrapped around herself like armour that had already failed.

No tears.

Just silence.

And that last line, echoing in her skull.
If you disappeared tomorrow, no one would even notice.

23

Part One: DI Tee and DC Zak

The office was silent except for the hum of the overhead light and the soft rustle of paper.

Detective Tee stood over the table, staring at the open file in front of her. For three days, the pieces hadn't quite fit. Now they were snapping into place with terrifying ease.

"Pause that there," she said.

The tech officer complied. The grainy security footage stuttered, then froze. Frame: Killer's figure outside the site where Tom's body was later found.

She zoomed in.

There, in the corner of the screen barely visible at first a shape in her hand.

"Can you enhance that?"

A few seconds of clicking. The shape resolved slightly. A syringe.

Another click. A glint of something darker on her sleeve.

"Blood?" Zak asked.

"Could be," the tech said. "Too degraded to confirm from this angle."

But it didn't matter. The timeline now matched the pathology report. Tom had died sometime between midnight and 2 a.m. on the same night killer was caught on camera.

Then came the phone logs. Burned SIM card. A hidden number pinged near the same coordinates. Registered to no one. Traced back to a burner phone that was later found in a bin behind the gym.

Part Two: Emma

I needed to keep digging into Lily's boxes, I needed to find out how bad it got for her. It was all just a joke, surely she should have seen that.

I found a new notebook, this one looked new.

Lily had hidden it behind the broken drawer in her closet —the one that stuck every time you tried to open it too fast. I wasn't even snooping. Not really. I was just looking for the charger we used to share.

But once I saw it, I couldn't pretend not to.

The notebook was black. Plain. No stickers, no name. Just a single word carved into the cover:

AFTERMATH

I sat on her bed and opened it.

The first page was a list.

Names.

Each one written in black ink.

Then some crossed out in red.

Tom.

Ben.

Maya.

Emma.

My breath caught.

I flipped to the next page. Paragraphs. Plans. Scenarios.

"Tom will be the first. His hands are dirty and he doesn't even know it. I want him to feel fear before he dies. Not because I enjoy it, but because he deserves to understand what I felt—cornered, helpless, waiting."

"Ben goes next. He always followed the loudest voice. Let's see what he does when there's only silence."

I felt my hands start to shake.

Then, another entry:

"Emma. I don't know yet. I want to forgive her. But every time I look in the mirror, I remember that she smiled while I disappeared."

My ears rang.

I turned the final page.

It was a map.

Red ink marking the construction site.

The gym.

Even our house.

At the bottom, written in the same cold handwriting:

"Justice isn't violence. It's clarity."

"But sometimes, clarity requires action."

I dropped the notebook.

*

I found her downstairs, drinking tea like nothing was wrong. Wearing my hoodie. Watching some old documentary she didn't even like.

I stood in the doorway, heart pounding.

She turned. Smiled.

But all I could see was the list. The ink. The plan.

My name.

"Emma?" she asked.

And suddenly I realised

She'd been watching me this whole time.

Waiting.

We'd both seen the same face in the mirror.

But only one of us had ever believed it was real.

Emma stood in the doorway of their shared bedroom, the tattered, spiral-bound notebook in her trembling hands. Her voice was low but cracked with fury and disbelief.

"What is this, Lily?" she demanded, flipping the pages to show Lily the jagged sketches, the lists of names, their names circled and crossed out with chilling precision.

"You wrote about killing us. You wrote about what you'd do, how you'd do it. You planned it."

Her eyes were wide, hurt and confusion spilling out of them. "Were you going to do it? Is that what this is? Were you going to hurt us?"

Lily sat frozen on the edge of the bed, pale and trembling, her breath caught somewhere between a gasp and a sob. "No," she whispered. "It wasn't real, Emma. I swear. I never meant… It was just writing, it was just… to get it out of my head. I never wanted to hurt you, not really."

Emma's hands shook as she threw the notebook onto the floor. "So what, you were just fantasising about killing your own sister and her friends?"

Lily buried her face in her hands, her shoulders shuddering. "You don't know what it's been like. The way you all treated me, like I was nothing. Like I didn't even exist. It was the only way I could make the thoughts stop."

Emma stared, silent now, her chest heaving. And then Lily said it, her voice barely audible, as if it had slipped out without permission. "It's not like with the cats. That was different." The air went still.

Emma blinked. "What?"

Lily's face went white. She clutched at the blanket beneath her like she could disappear into it. "I didn't mean" But it was too late.

"You killed the cats," Emma said, her voice dull with horror. "All those cats they were you?"

Lily tried to speak, to explain, but the words tangled in her throat. "I was angry. I didn't know how to stop it. They were... small. Helpless. Like I used to feel. I didn't think anyone would care. I didn't know it would get like this."

Emma backed away slowly, her face twisted with revulsion and grief. "Lily... what the hell have you done?" Lily stared at the notebook on the floor, the pages splayed open like a wound. "I didn't kill Sarah. Or Tom. I didn't. I hid the notebook because I knew what it looked like. But I didn't do that. I couldn't. I just wanted it all to stop."

Emma stumbled out of the room, her breath catching in her throat, the edges of her vision blurring. Her heart pounded so loudly it drowned out Lily's desperate voice calling after her. She couldn't look back. Couldn't see Lily's face again not now, not with the weight of that notebook still burning in her mind, those twisted, violent thoughts spelled out in ink like a confession.

She fumbled with the front door, her fingers clumsy and shaking. The second the cool evening air hit her skin, she gasped, like she'd been drowning in there and had only now come up for air. But there was no relief, only the roiling sickness in her stomach. She bent over on the front step, gagging, clutching the rail as if the world might spin her off without warning.

Lily. Her sister. Her *twin*. The person she'd grown up with, laughed with, shared every secret and every silence with was capable of *that*. Of killing animals. Of plotting violence, even if she swore it was just a release. Emma didn't know what was real anymore. Didn't know who her sister was.

And that terrified her more than anything.

She couldn't stay in that house. Not with those thoughts. Not with *her*. Emma backed away slowly, like Lily might appear at the door and pull her back in. Her legs carried her down the street before her mind could catch up, each step fuelled by a deep, primal instinct: get away. Just *get away*.

Because for the first time in her life, Emma didn't feel safe.

Not in her home.
Not with her sister.

Not even in her own skin.

24

Emma

Emma didn't stop running until her legs ached. Her breath came in short, shallow bursts, her chest tight with panic and disbelief. She couldn't go home not back to that house where her sister, her own flesh and blood, had written their deaths into a notebook like it was a script. Like it was inevitable.

She wandered until her feet brought her to the canal path, where the air was cooler, quieter. The sun was low, casting fractured orange light across the water. She sank onto a bench, burying her face in her hands. She didn't cry. She couldn't. Her mind was too busy spiralling through what she'd just seen.

Those pages. Those lists. Her name, etched in black ink and followed by cold deliberation. And Lily's face when she'd realised the truth had slipped out—about the cats. The calm way she'd said it, like it had been waiting to escape all along.

Emma tried to rationalise it. Lily hadn't killed Sarah or Tom she said that much. But the rest? The cruelty toward the animals? The detailed fantasy of revenge? It didn't just appear out of nowhere.

And then Emma began to wonder: if she hadn't found that notebook, how long would Lily have kept it all inside? What else was buried beneath her quiet exterior?

Back at the house, Lily sat frozen in the same position Emma had left her in, staring at the space Emma had vacated, as though the shadow of her still lingered.

Emma didn't know where to go, so she did the only thing she could think of. She called DC Zak.

He answered on the second ring. "Emma?"

Her voice cracked. "I think you need to come. It's about Lily."

*

Emma sat in the back of an unmarked car, her hands wrapped tightly around a warm tea someone had offered her. She hadn't touched it. She kept staring at the house at her childhood home now hollowed out by suspicion and fear.

Zak joined her in the car, quiet at first. Then, "What made you look in her room?"

Emma hesitated. "Something didn't feel right. I thought I could find... I don't know. Closure?"

Zak nodded slowly. "We're not saying she did what happened to Sarah or Tom. Not yet. But this changes things."

"I thought I knew her," Emma whispered. "We're twins. We used to finish each other's sentences. I never even knew she was hurting."

"She didn't want you to."

A long silence passed between them.

Finally, Zak asked, "Do you feel safe?"

Emma's answer was immediate. "No."

And that was all he needed to hear.

Because now they had more than suspicion.

They had intent. They had motive. And for the first time, they had a reason to fear what Lily might still be hiding.

And were they already too late to stop what was coming next?

25

The incident room had shifted from chaos to a haunted stillness. Walls once covered with sprawling evidence boards were now arranged with surgical precision, a grim mosaic of victims, suspects, timelines, and possibilities. DI Tee stood before it all, her arms folded tight against her chest, the quiet hum of the overhead lights the only sound besides the shuffle of DC Zak's notes.

Lily's notebook sat open on the table between them, pages splayed like a confession too raw to touch. Names. Crossed out in red. Paragraphs written in language that was eerily calm, clinical even. It had disturbed the entire team, not because it was proof but because it was nearly enough.

"She's unravelled," Zak said quietly, tapping his pen against the entry that described Tom's death in detail.

"Or she wants us to think that," Tee replied, eyes fixed on the timeline across the wall. "It reads like a script. But it doesn't match the actual kills. It's... messier in her head than it was in real life."

Zak turned, leaning his hip against the edge of the desk. "It's premeditation, Tee. Even if she didn't kill Sarah or Tom, this shows she thought about it. In detail. That alone puts her at the centre of this."

"But the MO is still wrong," Tee murmured. "Sarah's death was clean. Controlled. Calculated in a different way than this notebook suggests. And the blow that killed Tom one strike, perfectly placed. That's not the act of a teenage girl scribbling fantasies. That's someone with experience. Precision."

They sat in silence for a moment, the weight of what that implied thick in the air.

Then the phone rang.

Zak answered it with a clipped, "DC Zak," and listened. A moment later, his eyes widened, and he scribbled something onto the nearest notepad. "Where? How many? Okay. We're on our way."

He hung up and looked at Tee.

"Another call-out," he said grimly. "But this time it's not one cat. It's four. Dumped behind the school gym. Same area Sarah used to go to sketch. Same route Lily would've taken home."

Tee grabbed her jacket without a word. The storm wasn't just building now, it had broken.

*

The scene behind the gym was cordoned off when they arrived, the air heavy with the scent of refuse, rot, and something metallic that lingered too long in the back of the throat. Uniforms milled around the perimeter, but no one touched anything. Everyone knew now that these animal killings might be more than just cruelty.

Tee ducked under the tape and immediately spotted the cluster of lifeless bodies, cats, their fur matted with blood, bodies twisted and displayed in a deliberate pattern. Their necks had been broken. Not sloppily. Efficiently.

Zak crouched beside them, his face darkening.

"Arranged in a line," he said. "Each facing the gym. Whoever did this wasn't panicking. They took their time."

Tee knelt beside him, scanning the surrounding space. "These aren't like the first batch. There's no dismemberment. No post-mortem mutilation. It's almost clinical."

She stood and turned slowly, taking in the alley, the shadows, the view of the school buildings in the distance. "It's a message."

"To who?" Zak asked.

"To us," she said. "Or maybe to someone else. Someone who used to come here. Sarah. Lily. Even Emma."

A forensic officer approached, glancing down at the cats before looking at Tee. "No ID tags. But all appear to be domestic. These weren't strays. Someone lured them."

"Let me guess," Tee said. "No CCTV?"

"Not back here," the officer confirmed. "Blind spot."

Zak stood and brushed his hands off. "This doesn't match Lily's style, if we believe the earlier ones were hers. This is calculated, quiet. This feels like escalation."

Tee nodded slowly. "It also feels like someone trying to imitate Lily's work. Or build on it."

They exchanged a glance.

"It's not over," Zak said.

"No," Tee said. "It's getting started."

*

Lily's notebook, pages dog-eared and frantic, margins filled with erratic sketches and scribbled thoughts that shifted between guilt, fear, and confusion. The timeline a fragile thread of days and locations, fraying at the edges the harder they pulled.

The grainy CCTV footage: Sarah leaving the library alone. Tom walking the edge of the lake. The burner phone, unregistered, purchased in cash, pinging off nearby towers at strange, precise intervals.

The mutilated cats.

The ritualistic runes found in the clearing.

The diary entries with references to being watched, followed, hunted.

The emails Sarah had never sent drafts recovered from her school account, unsent messages that read more like confessions or warnings than anything else.

And then, Sarah's sessions with the counsellor.

Ms. Millfield.

Her name wasn't written in bold, wasn't underlined or circled. But it kept surfacing, in the margins, in footnotes, in casual mentions that suddenly didn't feel so casual. Her fingerprints weren't on anything, but her presence threaded through every part of Sarah's spiral. She had seen her regularly in the months before the disappearance. Sarah had stayed behind after lessons, cancelling plans with friends to meet in that quiet little office that smelled of lavender and old books. No one had thought much of it at the time just another student in need of support.

But now…

Now it felt significant.

She appeared in Lily's journal, once, barely noticeable, a single line: *"Millfield asked too many questions today. Think she suspects something."*
She was mentioned in the recovered emails Sarah thanking her for "listening, even when no one else would."

She was referenced in a group chat the night before Sarah vanished. Maya had sent a message: *"If she keeps pushing her to talk, she's going to say too much."*

Her voice was calm in the recordings. Measured. Kind. She was everything you'd expect a counsellor to be. But maybe… too perfect. Too consistent. Like someone who knew what to say because they were used to hiding in plain sight.

Tee sat back, brow furrowed, staring at the wall of evidence. It was a mess a web of trauma and lies and yet amid it all, one thread remained curiously intact.

Ms. Millfield.
"She was the last person Sarah spoke to in any depth before her death," Tee said. "The school said she's highly respected, deals with vulnerable teens. The kind of person

schools refer everyone to when they need to make a problem go away quietly."

"She helped Lily too," Zak added. "That's two victims with the same emotional outlet."

Tee narrowed her eyes. "Or two girls who were both handed over to the same gatekeeper. And then one ends up dead."

Zak turned slowly to her. "You think she's involved?"

"I think she knows more than she's telling."

He hesitated, then said, "You want to bring her in?"

"No," Tee said. "Not yet."

She closed the file on the desk.
"Let's talk to her again. This time, not as politely, before we bring in Lily. Something still isn't adding up."

26

Part One

Ms Millfield sat across from DI Tee and DC Zak, her expression composed but kind, her hands folded in her lap.

She looked tired.

"I understand how difficult this must be," she said gently. "I worked with Sarah for six months. Her death shook a lot of us."

Tee gave a polite nod. "We're hoping you can help us fill in some of the gaps Ms Millfield, particularly regarding Lily Shaw. We know she had a lot of sessions with you."

Sues brow furrowed with concern. "Oh please call me Sue. Yes, I saw Lily on and off over the past year. She was complex. Guarded, sometimes. But intelligent. Thoughtful. A lot of what she experienced at school left her raw."

"Did she ever express violent thoughts?" Zak asked.

She shook her head. "Not to me, no. She did talk about feeling powerless, and she sometimes wrote stories and journal entries as a way to cope, but that's common. It's a tool we encourage."

"And Sarah?" Tee asked.

A pause.

"Like I said before, she felt isolated," Sue said quietly. "More than I think anyone realised. She didn't just feel bullied she felt erased. Like she'd become invisible in her own life."

"Did she ever mention fear? Or anyone she felt unsafe around?"

Sue hesitated. "She mentioned names, yes. Some of the ones already under your radar. But she never suggested she was physically in danger. Emotionally... yes. Absolutely. Why are you asking me the same questions again?"

Zak nodded and ignored her question, scribbling something. "Why do you think no one acted?"

Sue exhaled slowly. "Because schools are overwhelmed. And because sometimes people think kids are just being dramatic. Sarah wasn't dramatic. She was drowning."

Tee met her gaze. "Thank you, Sue. That's helpful."

As they left, Sue rose to tidy the cushions on the couch. Her expression, briefly, turned distant, a flicker of sadness passing across her face before she tucked it away and reached for her clipboard.

DC Zak isn't convinced by Sue Millfield. Something about her story doesn't sit right, too rehearsed, too polished. Her eyes flickered just a little too quickly when he asked about her whereabouts that night, and while she played the concerned friend well, Zak sensed a deeper tension beneath the surface. He makes a note to dig deeper, background checks, financial records, phone logs. Whatever Sue is hiding, DC Zak intends to find it.

Part Two: The Arrest

Lily was in the garden when they arrived.

She had headphones in, sleeves rolled up, a spade in her hand, digging into the frost-bitten soil behind the shed. She looked up as the shadow fell across her — and saw Tee and Zak flanked by two officers.

There was a pause. No panic. No confusion. Just a slow, dawning understanding.

"Lily Shaw," Tee said clearly, "you are under arrest on suspicion of the unlawful killing of animals. You do not have to say anything, but it may harm your defence if you

297

do not mention when questioned something you later rely on in court. Anything you do say will be given in evidence."

Lily didn't argue. She placed the spade down carefully, like it might shatter if dropped.

Emma, watching from the kitchen door, gasped so hard it caught in her throat. She never thought something like this could happen, the betrayal, she had just sent her sister to prison.

Her twin silent, pale, let herself be led away.

Part Three: Lily in Custody

The grey walls of the interview room were blank, cold, suffocating in their stillness. The overhead light buzzed faintly, casting a harsh glare across the metal table bare, except for the thick file of evidence now open before her.

Lily sat opposite Tee and Zak, her wrists twitching slightly in her lap. Her face was pale, lips chapped, eyes sunken like she hadn't slept in days. But her voice, her voice was steady. Clear. Practised.

A solicitor sat beside her, arms crossed tightly, but Lily did most of the talking herself.

"I didn't kill Tom," she said flatly.

Tee watched her. "Then who did?"

Lily hesitated. Her jaw clenched. "I don't know. But someone wanted him dead more than I did."

Zak leaned in, pushing a photograph across the table the one they'd found in Lily's notebook. The runes. The sketch of Tom's face, crossed out.

"You wrote: 'I want him to feel fear before he dies.' That's not grief, Lily. That's not processing. That's premeditation."

"I was angry," Lily said quickly. "He let things happen. He stood by. But those were thoughts. Not actions."

Tee flipped another page. "'Justice requires clarity. Sometimes, clarity requires action.' That's another line from your notebook. Sound metaphorical to you?"

Lily's gaze dropped. Her fingers curled around each other in her lap.

"I was trying to understand it. What happened to Sarah. How nobody cared."

Zak didn't let up. "And the cats? Was that part of understanding, too?"

A pause. Heavier than the silence that had come before it.

"No," Lily admitted, voice cracking. "That was real. I did that."

"Why?" Tee asked.

Lily swallowed. "Because I couldn't scream. I couldn't cry in front of anyone. I needed control. And they were small, and easy to hurt, and they didn't fight back. I hated myself for it, but it gave me something to hold onto."

The solicitor finally shifted beside her, but said nothing.

Zak's tone was sharp. "We found animal blood in your bedroom. On your shoes. In your sketchbook. You weren't just hurting them, Lily. You were staging them."

Lily said nothing. Her eyes stayed down. Her silence was worse than any denial.

"And what about Sarah?" Tee pressed. "Your journal entries escalate right before her death. You talked about 'sacrifice,' 'rebalancing,' even described dreams of her lying in the woods. Dreams that almost exactly match how her body was found."

"I didn't kill her," Lily whispered. "I didn't want her dead. I just wanted… someone to listen."

"But she *was* found dead," Zak said. "And now Tom's gone too. And every road we follow seems to bring us back to you."

Tee leaned in, voice low and deliberate. "Lily, you're not just a troubled girl anymore. You're a suspect in two murder investigations. We have motive. We have opportunity. And we have a pattern of violence. If you know something, anything, now is the time to tell us."

But Lily stayed quiet.

Her hands trembled, but her eyes didn't meet theirs.

"I didn't kill them," she repeated, barely audible. "I just watched it all fall apart."

Tee straightened and closed the file with a soft thud.

"You're not going anywhere, Lily. Not yet."

As they stepped out of the room, Zak exhaled sharply. "She's not telling us everything."

"No," Tee agreed. "But it's not just her."

Zak frowned. "You think she had help?"

"I think," Tee said, eyes fixed down the corridor, "that someone's been pulling strings longer than we realised. And Lily might not be the puppet we assumed... but she's no bystander either."

Behind the one-way glass, Lily sat still in her chair. Watching the door.

Waiting.

And outside, the noose was tightening, not just around her, but around *all* of them.

27

DC Zak

Zak never liked loose ends and Sue Millfield felt like one. Not because she had said anything overtly suspicious during the interview, but because something didn't sit right.

It started with a line in her counselling notes. After re-reading the case files that evening, Zak noticed it not what she'd written, but how.

In one of Lily's files, there was a short observation: "Client displays traces of displaced retributive trauma, common among post-isolation adjustment cases."

Zak frowned.

That wasn't standard school counselling language. That was academic clinical. Graduate-level. Zak flagged it mentally. He knew the school only required a Level 4 counselling certificate to work with minors. But that language? That was someone with more than a certificate.

It was a thread.

And Zak started to pull it.

The next day, back at his desk with a mug of lukewarm coffee, Zak ran Sue Millfield through the national counselling registry.

She was listed.

Susan Ann Millfield. Registered with the British Association for Counselling and Psychotherapy (BACP), currently working freelance with schools and youth organisations. Licence number valid. Qualifications listed as expected foundation degree in counselling from a private college.

But one detail caught his eye.

Registration Year: 2019.

Zak frowned.

That was only six years ago. And yet in her interview, Sue had mentioned she'd been "working with vulnerable students for over fifteen years."

Maybe she'd misspoken.

Or maybe not.

He kept digging.

The school website had a staff profile page, minimal, just a headshot and title.
Zak downloaded it, then ran a reverse image search using internal police tools.

Most hits were dead ends.

Until one came from a cached university article: "Summer Millfield speaks on restorative psychology at Cambridge seminar, 2013."

The woman in the photo?

Same person.

Same high cheekbones. Same eyes. Same delicate scar near the chin.

Only the name had changed.
Zak's pulse picked up.

He cross-referenced the article with archived psychology directories. Summer J. Millfield, once a research fellow in adolescent psychology, had written three published papers in the early 2010s, all focused on trauma, shame, and retributive behaviour in teenagers.

Then, around 2015—nothing.

Gone.

No academic trails. No new papers. No public appearances.

She had vanished from the record.

And two years later, Sue Millfield appeared as a freelance school counsellor with a new BACP registration.

Zak checked the national archive database and police logs.

He filtered for Summer Millfield and sorted by incident reports between 2014 and 2016.

One result popped up.

A minor car accident in Kent, no injuries, but the name was logged. Summer Millfield. No other matches.

Then he dug deeper.

He called a contact in Records and asked for any name change filings linked to that name.

Ten minutes later, he had it.

Name Change Certificate – 2016: Summer Joan Millfield legally changed her name to Susan Ann Millfield. No listed marriage. Personal change.

Now Zak was fully alert.

He didn't know why she changed her name, not yet.

But someone doesn't walk away from a rising academic career in child psychology, scrub their name off the internet, and start again unless they're running from something.

And she hadn't just changed careers she'd buried an identity.

He pulled a full background check. This time, using Summer Millfield's name.

That's when he saw it.

A redacted incident from 2015.

A formal disciplinary hearing at the university she worked at. Details sealed, but keywords flagged:

Inappropriate boundaries. Breach of safeguarding protocol. Student complaint. Investigation dropped due to lack of evidence.

But the fallout? Summer resigned. Her papers were removed from public distribution. One journal withdrew a publication.

Zak sat back in his chair.

He didn't have everything yet.

But now he had a person of interest.
Sue Millfield or Summer was no longer just the kind, quiet counsellor.

She was someone with a secret.

And someone who had known all the victims personally.

He reached for his phone.

"Tee? I've found something you need to see."

28

Emma

The house still smelled like Lily. Vanilla lip balm and charcoal pencil shavings. That faint, almost bitter scent of the soy candles she was always burning but never finishing. Emma hadn't been able to bring herself to clean anything, not since Lily had been taken into custody. Mum and dad haven't spoken to each other, Dad is desperately trying to find a loop hole in the system. They haven't said it, but I know they blame me for not protecting her.

The silence felt surgical. A place cut clean open and left to bleed.

Emma sat on the floor in front of Lily's bookshelf, fingers resting on the edges of dog-eared journals and sketchbooks. She didn't know what she was looking for, only that she couldn't stop.

She was done pretending she didn't have questions.

Lily had said she hadn't killed Sarah or Tom. That the notebook was just her outlet, a scream on paper. Emma didn't believe everything... but part of her wanted to.

There was still something missing. A wrongness. Like she'd been staring at the picture upside down and hadn't noticed.

She pulled the last few books off the bottom shelf.
Nothing.

Except—

A folder. Grey. Plain. Taped shut along one side.

Lily's handwriting was scrawled across it: **Do Not Touch (I'll kill you).**

Emma let out a bitter breath. "Well," she muttered, "you sort of beat me to it."

She peeled the tape and opened the folder.

Inside were letters. Dozens. All addressed to one person.

Sue Millfield.

Each one was a different tone some pleading, some angry. Some Emma recognised as versions of things Lily had said out loud.

One caught her eye. It was dated two weeks before Sarah's death.

"You said people don't change. That they just get better at hiding what they are. But I'm not hiding anymore. If this is what being invisible makes me, then maybe I was right to stop trusting you."

Another, later one, was shorter. Almost a scrawl.

"I told you what Ben did. You did nothing. You always do nothing. Why do you let it happen?"

Emma's stomach twisted.

She knew Lily had confided in the counsellor—but she hadn't realised how deep it went. Or how angry Lily had been when nothing changed.

But it wasn't the letters that unsettled her most. It was what she found tucked between them.

A photo.

Worn. Old.

Two girls, maybe 15 or 16, sitting on a cracked wall in school uniforms. One had Lily's cheekbones, that same pointed chin but it wasn't Lily. This girl looked older. Early 2000s, maybe?

The other girl… Emma froze.

She knew that face.

It was Ms Millfield.

But younger. Much younger.

And smiling in a way Emma had never seen on her.
There was something written on the back.

"Me + Summer. Last day at St. Oswyn's. Finally free."

Summer.

Not Sue.

Emma stared at the name for a long time.

Summer.

Her fingers started to tremble.

Why would someone change their name and start again in
a new town unless they had something to run from?

She turned the folder over.

Another piece of paper fluttered loose and landed on the floor.

A photocopy of an article. Dated almost ten years ago. The headline was grainy, but the words chilled her blood.

"Psychologist Resigns Amid Allegations of Student Misconduct."

"Summer Millfield steps down from Cambridge-affiliated programme after a university inquiry into safeguarding failures. No charges filed."

Emma felt like the room tilted.

She read it again.

Millfield. Summer.

Sue Millfield had changed her name. And now she was back in schools, working with vulnerable kids. With Sarah. With Lily.

And no one had noticed.

No one had stopped her.

Emma picked up the photo again, and this time, she didn't see a quiet, well-meaning counsellor.

She saw someone watching.

Someone waiting.

And she realised something that made her skin crawl.

Lily had trusted Sue.

And Sue had been playing a long game.
Emma stood slowly, the article shaking in her hands.

She didn't know what this meant yet.

But she was going to find out.

And this time, she wasn't telling anyone, not until she knew exactly what Sue Millfield was hiding.

29

DI Tee and DC Zak

Zak's desk was a mess. Not like his usual organised and meticulous self, but this was born from obsession. Printouts, post-it notes, yellowing news clippings, a list of aliases scribbled in marker. And at the centre of it all: one name.

Summer Millfield.

DI Tee walked in holding a cup of vending machine coffee and froze when she saw his screen.

"You've barely left this office," she said. "Tell me you've got something real."

Zak stood, motioning her over. His eyes were bloodshot but sharp. "It's not a theory. It's buried, but I found her."

Tee narrowed her eyes. "Who?"

He pointed at the image on his monitor—an old article, partially scanned. A grainy photo of a younger woman flanked by lawyers.

"Sue Millfield's not who she says she is. Her real name's Summer Millfield. She changed it about eight years ago, legally, after a safeguarding investigation forced her resignation from a school-affiliated youth therapy programme."

He brought up the next document. "No charges were filed. The inquiry was internal. But two students made formal complaints about inappropriate boundaries. Emotional manipulation. Pressure to remain silent. She vanished after that—resurfaced three years later as Sue Millfield, private youth counsellor. And guess where she set up first?"

"St. Cedars," Tee said, her voice low.

Zak nodded. "It gets worse. The girls who made those complaints? One of them attempted suicide. The other dropped out and disappeared. I can't find a trace of her."

Tee's expression hardened. "And she got approved to work in schools again?"

"No one ever flagged it. With the name change and the time gap, she passed the DBS checks. No red flags. But she's been working with vulnerable teens ever since, including Sarah. And Lily."

Tee was quiet for a moment, then spoke with a chill edge: "That's a pattern."

"Yeah," Zak agreed. "One we missed."

She straightened up, jaw clenched. "Let's go to Lily. Now."

*

Lily — Custody Interview Room 3

Lily sat at the metal table in the interview room, pale but composed. Her wrists were cuffed to the steel loop embedded in the tabletop. Her hair was tied back, her hoodie replaced by grey custody-issue sweats. Her sketchbook was long gone, but her eyes were still full of the storm that had drawn them here in the first place.

Tee and Zak entered, a uniformed officer standing just outside the door.

Lily looked up. "More questions?"

Tee placed a slim folder on the table and sat opposite her. "Yes. And this time, we need you to listen carefully."
Lily didn't respond, but her gaze flicked to the folder.

Zak leaned forward. "We know about the notebook, Lily. We know what was in it. And we know how angry you were. But we also believe you when you say you didn't kill Sarah. Or Tom."

317

Lily's expression shifted slightly. Not quite relief—
something more cautious. "Why now?"

Tee opened the folder. Inside was a photo of Sue Millfield.
And next to it, an older one—clearly the same woman, but
younger, with the name Summer Millfield scribbled in the
margin.

"Because we think someone else was playing a bigger
game," Tee said. "And she got close to you when you were
at your worst."
Lily's lips parted slightly.

"She said she was trying to help."

Zak's tone was quiet. "She wasn't. Not in the way you
needed."

Lily's fingers curled into fists. "I told her things. Things I
never told anyone. She told me to 'focus the emotion.'
That it was okay to feel rage. That no one was going to
protect me but me."

"And did she ever... encourage you to write those plans
down?" Tee asked carefully.

Lily's throat moved. "She said it might help. She gave me a black notebook. Said to let it out there instead of in real life."

Tee and Zak exchanged a glance.

Lily looked from one to the other. "Are you saying… she set me up?"

Zak leaned in gently. "We're saying there's a possibility she saw what you were going through and she let it happen. Maybe even nudged it along."

Lily shook her head. "No… no, she couldn't. She was the only one who" She broke off, tears rising now, her control slipping.

Tee softened slightly. "You're not on your own anymore, Lily. But if we're going to get to the truth, we need to know everything. Did Sue, or Summer, ever mention Sarah? Tom? Did she ever talk about what they'd done?"

Lily nodded slowly. "She said they were toxic. That some people don't deserve closure. That pain only stops when it's been passed on."

Zak jotted the quote. "Passed on to who?"

Lily didn't answer. She just stared at the folder, her voice barely above a whisper.

"I thought I was the one breaking. But maybe she was the one already broken."

30

Part One: Emma

Emma hadn't planned on going into the attic, but she needed to dig deeper.

She'd been staying at her aunt's for the past three nights, living in a fog of shock and dread. She hadn't returned Lily's calls. Couldn't. Not after what she'd found the black notebook with its clinical tone, the pages dripping with barely-suppressed rage, and the quiet, accidental confession about the cats. But even in her silence, questions kept clawing at her from the inside out.

Lily wasn't lying.

She had said she didn't kill Sarah. Or Tom. She'd said it with the kind of hollow conviction that either meant she truly believed it… or she was a better liar than Emma had ever realised. But what unsettled Emma even more than the violence was the calmness. The way Lily had spoken as if she'd already made peace with everything she'd done. Like something, or someone, had helped her believe she was right to do it.

That's when the memory hit her a fragment, just before sleep the night before. Sue Millfield, or *Summer*, sitting in their kitchen two years ago, having tea with their mum. She'd brought a box of "old client records" and asked if she could store it in the attic during a home move. "Just for a month," she'd said.

No one had ever gone back for it.

Emma climbed the ladder slowly, her heart thudding with every creak of the rungs. The air up there was thick with dust and age, and the shadows seemed to lean toward her as she moved. She pulled her jumper tighter around her shoulders and shuffled aside a few old blankets and holiday boxes before she found it—pushed behind an unused fan heater and a broken vacuum.

A small, taped-up cardboard box.

She stared at it for a moment, her instincts screaming. Then she pulled it out and opened it.

Inside were several plain manila folders, each one labeled in neat black pen. Some held what looked like school reports. Others had notes—pages of counselling assessments written in a neat, orderly script.

But the deeper she dug, the more wrong it felt.

Hannah Kelson. Jamie Yeo. Mollie Finn.

Next to some names were circled words: *High risk. Withdrawn. Escalating self-harm. Susceptible to control.*

Emma's stomach churned. Her hands started to shake. One file held a photo of Hannah—barely fifteen in the picture. Next to it was a brief typed summary: *"Hannah Kelson. No guardian engagement. Student shows signs of dissociative episodes and displaced trust. Terminated sessions unexpectedly."*
Underlined in red: *"Location change recommended."*

Emma slammed the lid closed.

She didn't need to know any more.
She needed to *show* someone.

She was out of the attic and down the stairs before her thoughts could catch up, box pressed tight to her chest like it might try to escape. She didn't text Tee. She didn't call ahead.

She just *went*.

Part Two: The Station – Interview Room 5

The precinct was quieter than usual. Outside, dusk had settled into a steely grey, rain tapping softly at the windows. Zak sat hunched over a series of documents, his brow furrowed, when DI Tee walked in holding two coffee cups.

"Still no forensic confirmation from the locker sweep?" she asked.

Zak took one of the cups, shaking his head. "No, but I've got something better."

He pushed a printout across the desk. A certificate of deed poll.

"Sue Millfield legally changed her name in 2010. Original name: Summer Millfield. It was buried in the national register under an outdated school district entry. Took some digging."

Tee leaned over, scanning the form. "Any reason given?"

Zak shrugged. "Just 'personal circumstances.' But here's the kicker—before she became Sue, Summer was linked to two separate schools where students had breakdowns... or disappeared. One school in Devon. One in Leeds. Same pattern. Vulnerable students. Gaps in records. Early exits."

"Any direct complaints?" Tee asked.

"Nothing documented," Zak said. "But I cross-referenced three names from Lily's old counselling logs with school safeguarding reports. All three students were seen by Summer Millfield during key escalation periods."

Tee ran a hand through her hair. "And now two kids are dead, one's in custody, and somehow Sue Millfield's been inside the system for over a decade without a red flag."

Zak's response was cut short by a knock at the glass door. A young constable poked her head in, breathless. "Sir? Ma'am? There's someone downstairs. Says she has urgent evidence relating to the counsellor. Emma Shaw."

Tee and Zak froze for half a second.

"Bring her up," Tee said sharply.

Emma looked soaked when she entered, rain slicking the tips of her fringe. She was clutching a cardboard box tightly to her chest, knuckles white.

"I found this in our attic," she said, placing it on the table. "She gave it to our mum years ago, said it was just old paperwork. But it's not. It's" Her voice caught. "It's everything."

Tee opened the box. Zak pulled the files free, laying them out one by one.

Dozens of student profiles. Some with detailed notes. Many marked "ESR"—Emma asked what it meant. Tee didn't answer. She already knew.

Emotionally Susceptible and Reactive.

A term used in risk modelling. In practice, it meant "easy to manipulate."

Zak flipped through one folder, eyes narrowing. "Hannah Kelson. She was flagged in that cold case file from Leeds. Disappeared six years ago. No remains found."

Emma nodded. "She's in Lily's journal too. Just mentioned in passing. Said she was one of the girls that 'Sue wouldn't talk about anymore.'"

Tee looked up. "She's not Sue. Her real name's Summer. Summer Millfield."

Emma blinked, the colour draining from her face. "She's been lying... all this time?"

Zak nodded grimly. "We need to get to Leeds, talk to Hannah Kelsons old school, someone at that school should remember something."

31

Emma

Emma sat in the narrow waiting area of the station, staring blankly at the cracked tile floor. The hum of overhead lights mingled with the occasional buzz of distant phones and the muffled voices of officers behind closed doors. But in Emma's head, there was only static.

She didn't feel like a hero.

She didn't feel brave, or strong, or clever.

She felt... cracked. Splintered into pieces she couldn't quite hold together. Like she'd pushed over a stone and found rot underneath it, something festering and deeper than she ever imagined.

The box she'd brought in was still somewhere inside—likely tagged as evidence now, being catalogued and dissected like her entire childhood.

A counsellor. Trusted by the school. By her family. The woman who sat at their kitchen table drinking peppermint tea and complimenting Lily's drawings. The woman who hugged their mum after Sarah's funeral. The woman who, somehow, had wormed her way into the heart of everything.

And Emma had helped expose her.

But it didn't feel like victory.

She kept going back to Lily.

Her sister. Her twin. They'd shared everything once—the same room, the same clothes, the same birthday cake every year. And now Emma didn't know if they shared anything at all.

The notebook still haunted her. The language, the cruelty. The way Lily had written about her "She smiled while I disappeared."

Emma didn't remember smiling. But maybe that was the problem.

She had disappeared for a while. Into popularity. Into safety. Into a version of herself that didn't ask questions. While Lily… drowned.

A lump rose in her throat, heavy with guilt and confusion. She didn't know whether to scream, cry, or call their mum.

What if she'd noticed sooner?

What if she'd actually asked Lily how she was? Not in passing, not the way you ask someone when you expect them to lie, but really asked?

Maybe the notebook wouldn't exist.

Maybe the cats would still be alive.

Maybe Tom and Sarah would too.

She wiped a tear from her cheek, then realised she was shaking.

An officer approached her gently, holding out a paper cup of water.

"Miss Shaw? The detectives said they'll be a little while. You're welcome to wait as long as you need."

Emma nodded mutely, clutching the water without drinking. "Thanks."

The officer hesitated. "I read your statement," she said quietly. "I know you probably don't feel it right now... but what you did? Coming in here, bringing that evidence? That mattered. A lot."

Emma gave a strained nod, but she didn't answer. She wasn't sure what she believed anymore.

She thought of the time someone, she can't remember who, had pulled Emma aside after gym class, eyes darting. "Lily's not okay," she'd said. "Someone should talk to her." Emma had shrugged it off. Everyone said that.

Emma closed her eyes and let her head fall back against the cold wall behind her.

Memories weren't supposed to come like this—sharp, jagged, invasive. But they did. And once they started, she couldn't stop them.

Lily in Year 10. Quiet, bookish, always scribbling in the margins of her notebook. Hair a little too long, jumper sleeves pulled over her hands like armour.

Emma remembered laughing.

Not at something Lily said.

But at Lily herself.

It had started so casually. A comment in the hallway, tossed out like gum.

"Could you look any more tragic?"

She hadn't meant it. Not really. She was just tired. Or annoyed. Or trying to be funny in front of Tom and Ben.

But Lily had gone silent. Her eyes didn't narrow or roll. They just… dimmed.

Emma remembered that.

She remembered how it made her feel strong.

After that, it got easier.

Small digs at the dinner table.

"She's always in her room. Probably hexing us."

Or in front of friends:

"Don't worry about Lily. She's just... like that."

She used to swap Lily's books from her bag when she wasn't looking. Hide her sketchpads. Once, she told their form tutor Lily was skipping homework on purpose, knowing full well her sister had spent the weekend drawing until her fingers cramped.

Lily never told.

Not once.

Not even when Emma borrowed her favourite hoodie and spilt paint on it and pretended not to know where it went.

Lily had simply stopped wearing hoodies after that.

The worst memory came from a party. Someone had dared Emma to show a video from Lily's room—one she secretly recorded of Lily singing softly to herself, off-key, head swaying. It was nothing. Harmless.

But when she showed it around, people laughed.

And Lily found out.

She didn't cry. She didn't scream.

She just didn't speak to Emma for a week.

Emma had told herself Lily was being dramatic.

But now, sitting in a police station, with a notebook full of her sister's darkest thoughts echoing through her skull, she knew the truth.
She hadn't been dramatic.

She had been breaking.

And Emma had watched it happen, step by step, and kept walking.

Emma's phone buzzed quietly in her pocket. A message from her aunt, asking if she was alright.

She didn't reply.

She sat there, still, until the hallway emptied. Until the fluorescent lights buzzed too loudly. Until the weight of everything she hadn't done became too loud to bear.

But underneath it all, something had shifted. A new sense of responsibility—heavy, unwelcome, but real.

Emma couldn't undo what had happened.

But maybe she could be the kind of sister Lily once needed.

Maybe it wasn't too late to start showing up.
Not just for Lily.

But for herself, too.

*

The shame in her chest twisted into something else. Something harder. Sharper. Rage.
Not at Lily. Not anymore.

At *her*.

Summer Millfield. Or whatever her real name was. The counsellor.

The one person Lily had trusted when no one else listened.

The adult who had written the reports, taken the notes, nodded kindly and said words like *safe space* and *support system.*

And yet, somehow, all of this had still happened.

And Emma couldn't shake the feeling that Summer had known more than she ever said.

Why hadn't she sounded the alarm? Why hadn't she pushed harder when Lily started slipping?

Emma stood abruptly, her hands balled into fists. The weight of her guilt had become fuel. She couldn't fix what she'd done to Lily. She couldn't take back the cruelty or the silence. But she could get answers.

She could look Summer Millfield in the eye and ask *why.*

Why didn't you stop this?

Why didn't you save her?

Emma grabbed her coat and headed for the door, her jaw clenched.

It was time someone held that woman accountable. Even if no one else had the guts to do it.

She wasn't scared anymore.

She was *furious*.

And she wasn't leaving without the truth.

32

DI Tee and DC Zak

The sky over Leeds was the colour of wet slate, heavy with unspent rain. The train had pulled in just after eleven, and by the time DI Tee and DC Zak stepped through the rusted gates of St. Balthazar's School, the clouds hung low enough to taste.

It was a redbrick building, long and hunched, the sort of place that clung to the edges of the city like a memory it didn't want to keep. A place caught between too many pasts and not enough present.

Zak shoved his hands in his coat pockets as they walked. "Looks like the kind of place kids come out worse than they went in."

Tee didn't respond. She was already scanning the courtyard the worn benches, the vandalised bin, the cracked concrete underfoot. Every detail spoke of neglect, but also familiarity. This place hadn't changed much in a decade. She'd seen schools like this before: tired, overworked, always one bad year away from an Ofsted report that gutted what little funding they had left.

They were led inside by a receptionist with watery eyes and a permanent whisper in her voice. The headteacher,

Mr. Patrick Colgrave was waiting just outside his office, a gaunt man in his sixties with thinning grey hair and a handshake that felt too firm for his frame.

"I remember her," he said before they'd even sat down. "Hannah Kelson. It's not the kind of name you forget."

Tee pulled out her notebook, already writing. "We understand she was a student here from 2012 to 2019?"

Colgrave nodded, motioning toward a pair of worn chairs across from his desk. "Yes. Troubled. Very bright, but isolated. From what I recall, she didn't speak much, until she started seeing Ms. Millfield."

Tee's pen stopped. "Why would you mention Ms. Millfield?"

Colgrave gave a tight smile. "Every Wednesday. She was brought in as part of a council initiative on youth mental health. Rotated between several schools, but she spent a lot of time with us. Something about her never sat well with me, but without any proof nobody would listen. I had nothing to go off, just an instinct."

Zak tilted his head. "And she worked closely with Hannah?"

"Too closely, if I'm honest." Colgrave's smile faded. "I'll be frank. There was something... intense about their dynamic. Hannah changed after she started those sessions. She'd always been withdrawn, but suddenly she became well, not violent, exactly. Just... sharp. Like all her emotions had gone from numb to razor-edged."

Tee leaned forward slightly. "Did you raise concerns at the time?"

"I did." Colgrave rubbed the bridge of his nose. "But Sue Millfield had a way of disarming you. She spoke with authority, but always gently, always just enough to make you question your own instincts. She said Hannah was 'processing trauma' and that anger was part of the healing. She assured us it was under control."

"Was it?" Zak asked.

Colgrave hesitated. "Three months before Hannah left the school, another girl, Aimee Gilston was found unconscious in the gym toilets. No evidence of a fight, no witnesses. But she wouldn't talk. Neither would Hannah. And that was the end of it. She has also been seeing Ms. Millfield."

Tee's stomach turned. The pattern was there again. An isolated girl. A quiet, charismatic counsellor. And then, a violent break no one dared name.

Zak flipped open a tablet and pulled up the archived file. "Hannah Kelson then disappeared, is there anything you can tell us about that?"

Colgrave swallowed. "I don't think I can be of any help with that. But I'm not surprised. She was lost, that girl. And Sue—" He paused. "She made her feel seen. Heard. But I often wondered if she'd handed her a mirror or a match."

Tee tapped her pen against her notebook. "Did Sue Millfield keep any records? Session notes?"

"She did. But when she stopped working here, she took them with her. Said it was a confidentiality issue, since she operated under an external authority. We didn't argue."

"Do you remember anything else unusual?" Zak asked.

Colgrave hesitated. Then said, "There was one thing."

They both looked at him.

"Just before she left, Hannah gave one of our younger students a note. Slipped into her locker. We only found it because her mother reported it to the school it said: They watch us when we cry. It was written in black ink, but the words were circled with red pen. Careful, deliberate loops. Very similar to something she'd written on a poster in her form room a few weeks earlier."

Tee felt a chill settle down her spine. It was familiar. Too familiar.

"Do you still have the note?" she asked.

Colgrave stood. "No I'm sorry, as you can imagine it was a long time ago now."

As he left the room, Zak turned to Tee. "That's two girls. Same voice whispering in their ears."
Tee nodded slowly. "And we ignored the first until it was too late."

Zak exhaled. "She's not just a counsellor."
Tee stared at the chair where Colgrave had sat. Her hands were still, but her jaw clenched.
"No," she said. "She's a curator."

"Of what?"

Tee looked down at her notes.

"Of grief. Rage. And girls who no one listened to."

Tee rose from the table. "That's enough. We get the warrant. We bring her in. ASAP."

33

Emma

The door creaked open before Emma's knuckles made contact for the second time. Summer Millfield stood framed in the hallway, her expression calm, almost too calm. Like she'd been expecting this, waiting for it. In the soft light spilling from behind her, she looked smaller somehow, her neat cardigan buttoned to the top, tartan slippers, a delicate porcelain teacup in one hand. But it was the stillness in her eyes that made Emma hesitate. Something about it was off. Hollow.

"I wondered when you'd come back." Summer said softly, voice almost kind. "You look tired."

Emma didn't answer. She brushed past her into the hallway without being asked, her hands shaking, her heart pounding in her chest like a siren. The warmth of the office lavender-scented, filled with soft lamps and old furniture, made the horror more surreal. A predator shouldn't live somewhere so gentle.

"Sit down, if you like," Summer offered, closing the door. "I'll make tea."

"Don't," Emma snapped. "No more pretending."

Summer's eyebrow rose slightly, but she said nothing. She moved with grace into the living room and took her usual place in the old armchair, as if Emma were just another troubled student visiting for a pastoral chat. Emma dropped the notebook onto the coffee table. It hit with a dull slap, pages marked and dog-eared, a mess of pain and obsession.

"You knew," Emma hissed. "You knew what Lily was writing. You encouraged it."

"I never encouraged anything," Summer said calmly, folding her hands in her lap. "That notebook was private. An outlet. I told her to explore her emotions honestly. You'd be amazed how many people fantasise about revenge, Emma. That doesn't mean they act on it."

"But she did. Or... you did." Emma's voice cracked. "Tom. Sarah."

Summer said nothing.

Emma took a step forward, her eyes wild. "You killed them, didn't you?"

A long pause. The air thickened between them.

Then: "Yes," Summer said simply, her voice almost apologetic. "I killed Sarah. I killed Tom."

The room tilted sideways. Emma grabbed the back of the armchair to steady herself.

"Why?"

Summer's breath escaped her like it had been waiting years to be released. "Because Sarah deserved peace. She didn't get to grow past what you all did to her. She was already broken by the time she came to me. And Tom..." She trailed off, her eyes distant. "Tom was worse. Loud, smug, cruel in that effortless, public schoolboy way. I saw the way he laughed while your sister shrank. I saw the way you all looked away. No one protected her. Not even you."

Emma's throat closed up. "You murdered two teenagers."

"And yet Lily's in a cell," Summer said quietly.

Emma's hands clenched into fists. "You used her."

"I protected her," Summer said, leaning forward slightly. "I gave her language for her pain. A place to put it. I never wanted her to act on it. I just wanted her to see that she wasn't alone. That her fury made sense. That what was done to her mattered."

"You told her to kill me," Emma said hoarsely. "Don't lie."

"I told her," Summer said softly, "to decide who she wanted to be. If she couldn't forgive you, I said she needed to face that. Confront it. Whatever that meant to her. She wrote it down. She practiced on animals yes, that was wrong but she never crossed the line. I was the one who did."

Emma took a step back, tears building.

"You pushed her toward murder... and killed others in her name?"

"She needed to feel seen," Summer said, a sad smile touching her lips. "And when I realised just how deep she was sinking... how fractured she was becoming... I tried to take the burden myself. To do the thing she couldn't. To make the world pay the debt it owed her."

Emma shook her head violently. "You're sick."

"I'm pragmatic," Summer said evenly. "And I cared more about Lily's soul than anyone else ever did."

A long silence.

Then, Summer's voice dropped. "You're here because you're scared. Because deep down, you still don't believe her. And you shouldn't."

Emma's breath hitched. "She's my sister."

"She was," Summer said gently. "Now she's something else. A scar walking around in skin. You don't know the half of what she wrote. What she fantasised about. What she planned."

"She didn't kill Sarah," Emma said, trying to ground herself in something solid.

"No," Summer admitted. "That was me. But Lily was preparing for you."

Emma blinked, blood draining from her face. "What?"

"That was always the plan. She didn't have the nerve in the end... or maybe she just wanted you to suffer in a different way. But she wrote it all down. She rehearsed it. In her head. In her dreams. That fury never went away, Emma. You need to know that."

Emma staggered back. "Why are you telling me this?"

"Because," Summer said softly, "you need to find the recording. The last session. It's hidden in the vent at the back of my desk. I recorded it without her knowing. I was scared. I needed to document what she was saying."

Emma's eyes filled. "What's on it?"

Summer gave a tired smile. "Everything. The truth. About what she felt. What she saw. What you didn't see."

Emma reached toward the fire poker by the hearth. Her hands trembled.

"No more games."

Summer stood slowly, unafraid.

"I didn't think it would be you," she murmured.

Emma swung.

The metal cracked against flesh. Summer collapsed to the floor, her cup shattering beside her. Blood spilled across the rug in thick, rhythmic pulses. Her breath came in wet, ragged bursts.

Still, she looked up. Calm. Unmoving.

"I'm sorry," she whispered. "I never wanted her to become like me."

Emma dropped to her knees, sobbing. "You're a monster."

Summer coughed, blood painting her lips. "And yet... you killed me."

Emma froze.

Summer's smile was faint, fading. "You need to listen to the last recording... in the vent... Lily's last session."

"Why?" Emma breathed.

"Because she didn't kill Sarah," Summer rasped, "but she did... practice... for you."

Emma's world collapsed.

"What?"

"That was always the plan."

Summer exhaled one last time. Her chest stilled. Her eyes closed.

She was gone.

Emma knelt in the bloody quiet, shaking, surrounded by the final truth. The one she'd avoided. The one that now lived inside her chest like a ticking bomb.

She had to find that recording.

She had to know, once and for all, what her sister had planned.

34

DI Tee and DC Zak

The warrant was signed and sealed by 08:07.

The signature still glistened faintly, ink not yet fully dry.

Tee stared down at it, reading the words again even though she already knew them by heart. Her thumb pressed hard into the corner of the page, creasing it slightly, as if she could absorb its authority—its weight—into her own bones. This wasn't just protocol anymore. It wasn't just another line item in a case file.

This was a reckoning. Long overdue. And personal.

She could feel it in the tightness behind her eyes, in the knot that had taken up residence in her chest since the moment the pieces began to fit together. The lies. The manipulation. The careful, smiling face behind the violence. A counsellor. A protector. Someone meant to catch the broken ones before they fell too far.

Tee felt sick.

She glanced across the table at Zak. He was already zipping up his field bag, movements brisk, methodical. His jaw was tight, his usual sarcasm replaced by a quiet tension she recognised all too well he was angry. Righteously so.

"She's not going to run," Zak said, breaking the silence. "People like her think they're untouchable."

Tee folded the warrant carefully, sliding it into the document wallet and snapping it shut with more force than necessary. "They always do. Right up until the cuffs go on."

Zak nodded. "We good to move?"

Tee exhaled, straightened. She adjusted the strap of her vest, her badge already clipped in place.

"Yeah," she said. "Let's end this."

And with that, they stepped out into the morning light—warrant in hand, truth finally within reach.

The drive to Summer Millfield's office address was short, quiet. The sort of neighbourhood where curtains were drawn on weekend mornings and the air always smelled faintly of someone's toast.

But there was no smoke from Summer's chimney. No radio murmuring from the kitchen window like there usually was.

They pulled up to find the street undisturbed. No movement inside the house. The curtains stayed still.

"She's in there," Zak muttered, more hope than certainty.

Tee radioed the team. "Units two and three, approach from the rear and north side. We go on command."

At the door, they knocked once. Then again. Loud, firm.

"Police! Ms. Millfield, open the door!"

Nothing.

One of the uniformed officers stepped forward with the ram. A single, precise swing—and the front door burst inward with a crack.

Tee drew her weapon.

Inside, the house was cold.

Still.

Too still.

They cleared it room by room. The kitchen had two half-washed mugs in the sink. A blanket was folded neatly on the arm of the sofa. Nothing screamed struggle.

Until they reached the lounge.

Zak saw the blood first.

"Here!"

Tee turned the corner and froze.

Summer Millfield lay motionless, sprawled beside the coffee table. The blood beneath her had dried dark into the fibres of the carpet. A jagged wound curved from behind her ear to her temple. No sign of a defensive struggle. Just… execution.

Tee crouched beside the body, taking in the scene. "Approximate time?"

"Between 10pm and 1am," one of the on-scene medics said. "She was dead before we woke up."

Zak rubbed a hand down his face, stepping back. "We missed her by hours. If only that warrant came through sooner."

"No forced entry," another officer added. "Nothing broken. Someone she let in, or someone with a key."

Tee looked around the room—at the scattered notepads, the carefully arranged bookshelf, the tea-stained coaster on the side table.

"She was expecting someone."

Zak's brow furrowed. "Who would have done this, Emma? She did abruptly leave the station."

Tee hesitated. "We don't speculate yet. We prove."

*

In the back office, one of the forensic techs called out. "Detectives!"

Tee and Zak stepped in as he gestured toward the floor vent, half-removed. "This grate had fresh markings. We checked inside."

From the cavity, he held up a small flash drive in an evidence bag.

"No label," he said. "But someone wanted it hidden."

Tee took it carefully. "Get it back to the station. High priority processing."

Zak stood near the window, looking out into the quiet street. "You think it's her insurance policy?"

Tee didn't answer immediately.

Her eyes shifted toward the hallway, then back to Summer's lifeless form.

"Whatever it is," she said, "she wanted us to find it."

35

Emma

I hadn't meant to kill Summer Millfield.

But once the blood dried, and the silence thickened like a noose around both our necks, my intentions didn't matter. Not anymore.

I stood over her body too long, frozen. Blinking through the haze, the heat pounding behind my eyes, her blood cooling at my feet. The room smelled like cold tea and rusty metallic, sour, final.

I'd come looking for answers, but what I got was something else entirely. A confession. A poison, poured slow and steady down my throat.

Sarah.

Tom.

Summer had killed them both. But that wasn't even the worst of it. The worst part was Lily.

What Summer had stirred to life in her.

"She practised on the cats," she whispered, blood slick on her lips. "But it was always meant to be you."

I dropped the fire poker. Stumbled back. My whole body shaking. I pressed my hand to my mouth to stop myself from being sick. My ears were ringing. My vision blurred. The words echoed over and over again.

Lily.

My Lily.
The quiet one. The awkward one. My twin.

My would-be murderer.

There hadn't been a plan. Just instinct—twisted, sharp, burning in my chest like fury and fear had fused into one.

I couldn't stay. But I couldn't run forever either. Someone would find Summer's body. Maybe a neighbour. Maybe the postman. The police would come. And the story would write itself: *Sister of prime suspect murders respected counsellor in sudden rage.*

Only she wasn't just a counsellor.

And Lily... Lily wasn't just broken.

I needed someone to see that. To *understand.*

So I went to the study. My hands were trembling. My vision was going in and out, like a dream I couldn't wake from. But I remembered what she'd said—*the vent, behind the desk.* I found it. Behind the plaster and insulation, wedged tight, was the flash drive. I didn't even need a screwdriver. I used the corner of a book to pry the vent open and reached in.

I held the drive in my palm for a long time. I could take it. Run. Use it to clear my name. But something twisted inside me. They wouldn't believe me, not if I was the one holding it. Not if I was the one who had killed her.

It had to look like Summer had left it for herself. Like it had always been meant to be found. So I pushed it back into the vent. Not hidden this time. Just visible, half-sticking out, like a mistake. I knocked a picture frame loose nearby, just enough to draw attention.

A breadcrumb.

They'd find it. And when they did, everything would shift. I left the house just as the sun was rising. The sky bled streaks of grey and pink across the horizon like bruises. I didn't take my phone. I smashed it in a bin behind a petrol station an hour later.

Did she hate my face? Did she practise watching me die?

I told myself not to cry. I tried.

But the sobs came anyway silent, choking, pressed into my hands as the train rolled farther and farther from the life I thought I had.

I hadn't just lost my sister.
I'd lost the only version of my childhood that ever felt like it might have been real.

*

Back at the station, the atmosphere was dense with anticipation. DC Zak moved quickly through the corridors, the USB drive gripped tightly in his fist. He didn't stop for chatter or coffee or protocol—just stormed into the tech suite.

"Get this to analysis. Now," he snapped. "I want it open and playing in five minutes."

A tech officer spun toward him, catching the urgency. "On it."

He inserted the USB into the terminal, fingers flying over the keyboard. Lines of code filled the screen. Zak hovered over his shoulder, breath shallow.

Then the tech paused.

Zak leaned forward. "Problem?"

The tech shook his head slowly. "It's already decrypted. Just one file. Audio. Dated two days before Summer's death."

Zak straightened. "Play it."

He didn't wait to hear it himself. Instead, he walked fast through the station toward the main floor, where DI Tee had just arrived—coat half-on, hair knotted, dark circles under her eyes.

He held out the headphones. "You need to hear this."

Tee didn't ask questions. She put the headphones on.

And listened.

Click. Static. Then Lily's voice, calm and hollow.

"I think about Emma the most…"

"I don't know if that makes me sick. Or sane. Maybe I already decided to. Maybe I did a long time ago."

357

A pause. Then Summer's voice—smooth, professional, almost warm:

"You can say it here, Lily. You're safe. This is your space."

"No one's going to judge you."

Lily hesitated, then spoke again:

"I want her to see me. Not just look at me. I want her to *understand* it's her. That I chose her."

"I dream about her face... when she knows what's happening. That moment of realisation."

Summer's voice came again, lower, softer.

"Good. That clarity is important."

"And the animals? The cats?"

Lily paused. Then:

"It helped. I had to try it. To know what it felt like."

Summer gave a small laugh not cruel, not mocking. Something worse. Encouraging.

"That was brave, Lily. That was growth. You took control of your story."

"Most people never get past the fantasy stage."

"You stepped into it."

Lily's voice lowered.

"I didn't want them to suffer."

"But I needed to feel what it would be like. What it would take."

Summer's voice was a thread of approval, coated in syrup:

"That's what we talked about, isn't it? Control. Clarity. Practice."

"You didn't run from the feeling. That's important. You're further along than you think."

Silence. A breath. A shift of clothing against upholstery.

Then Lily again:

"She won't scream. Not at first. She'll be confused. She always has to figure things out before she reacts."

359

"But I want her to scream. I want her to *know*."

"This is for everything she pretended not to see. All the times she let me fade."

Summer's voice was a near-whisper now soothing, proud:

"That's it, Lily. Don't run from it. Say it aloud. Say what you want."

"I want her to *feel it*."

"And I want it to be *slow*."

Tee ripped the headphones off. Her pulse roared in her ears. Her hand trembled where it hovered over the desk.

Zak stood still, watching her. "She left that for us," he said softly. "Emma. She knew it was the only way we'd believe her."

Tee's voice was quiet. Hollow. "And now she's gone."

Zak didn't have to say it. They both knew.

She hadn't run out of guilt. She'd run because the truth was too sharp, too unbelievable.

And now they weren't chasing a killer.

They were chasing the end of something that had been *allowed* to grow. Nurtured.

Sanctioned.

By someone who wore a cardigan and smiled while girls cracked open from the inside.

*

In the abandoned house just off the quarry, Emma sat on the dusty, mouldy bed, knees drawn to her chest. Her hair hung damp around her face, the brown tint patchy in the flickering bathroom light.

The news was already rolling out on the TV in the background:

Local counsellor found dead. Police launch investigation. Sources confirm a connection to the ongoing murder case of Sarah and Tom..

No mention of Emma's name yet. But it would come. She had no illusions. She had killed Summer Millfield. No jury would care about why. But she also knew the USB would change everything. They'd listen. They'd hear what she'd heard. And they'd know what her sister really was.

Emma stood slowly, staring at her reflection in the smeared mirror. For the first time, she didn't look like a victim. Or a bully. Or a sister.

She just looked like someone who had seen too much. The kind of person who couldn't go home again. And maybe didn't deserve to.

36

Lily

They told her time passed differently in custody. That the hours blurred, that the walls began to breathe with your thoughts, feeding them back to you louder than before. But she didn't need a holding cell to understand how time stretched. She'd felt it for years, ever since St Cedars, ever since that first whisper of laughter behind her back. Time had never been linear for her. It curled. It dug in. It rotted.

Now, alone in the sterile silence the cell, it wrapped around her throat.

She lay curled on the narrow bed, her arms tucked around her knees, her body still aching from the endless hours of questioning. Her lips were dry. She hadn't cried, not yet, not in front of them. But inside, something was slipping. And she wasn't sure she could hold it in anymore.

They thought they knew everything.

Emma. The detectives. They had the notebooks, the drawings, the interviews, the threats. They thought that was the full picture, the angry little sister, quiet and strange, who never really fit in, who snapped one day and started tearing at the fabric of their perfect lives.

They were wrong.

Yes, she'd written the plans. Yes, she'd imagined the revenge. And yes, she'd killed the cats. She could never take that back. But it wasn't what they thought it was. It had never been about carnage. It was about *feeling*. After years of numbness, it was a grotesque kind of control. A way to rehearse the pain before someone else gave it to her again.

But Tom? Sarah?

She hadn't done that.

Lily bit down on the edge of her sleeve, tasting cotton and salt. She hated the room — its clean, cold edges. She hated the mirror that watched her constantly, like the eye of some god who didn't believe her either.

Emma thought she was a monster.

That cut deeper than anything.

Emma, with her pretty hair and easy laugh, who everyone liked instantly. Who played the ringleader without even noticing. Who joined the mockery without once realising she was laughing at her own twin. Emma, who now believed she was capable of killing. Who had *run away* instead of asking her why.

She didn't blame her. Not fully.

That was the worst part.

She had wanted Emma to feel it. To feel *something*. To understand, for just a moment, what it was to be invisible — to scream without a sound, to break without anyone noticing.

But now?

Now there were real bodies.

Real blood.

Real questions that wouldn't go away.

And Summer, kind, perceptive. Summer was dead.

Lily didn't even know yet how. The guards had been tight-lipped. But it didn't matter. She *knew*. There was a hole inside her chest where the only adult who'd ever listened used to live.

She didn't know what had happened. But she could guess. Emma had been spinning, falling, desperate for answers. And Summer... Summer had secrets of her own. Lily had always felt it, even before she could name it.

She sat up slowly, pushing the heels of her palms into her eyes until stars bloomed. Her breath came hard. There was no one to talk to. The detectives had said they'd be back. DC Zak had looked at her like he wanted to believe her, but he didn't.

Tee just wanted to punish her somehow. Tidy. Solved.

But the story wasn't tidy, Lily didn't actually kill anyone.

Lily dropped her feet to the floor. Cold tile. The click of the overhead light. Her eyes burned. She tried to remember what she'd said in the appointments. What Summer might've recorded. Would it help her? Hurt her? Had she said too much — or not enough?

But Lily had nothing else left.

Nothing except the truth.

And the truth was this:

She had wanted revenge.

She had fantasised about it.

She had even prepared.
But she hadn't killed Sarah.

She hadn't touched Tom.

And if someone had convinced Emma otherwise, if *Summer* had whispered poison into her ear, then Lily was more alone than she'd ever been before.

A knock rattled the metal door.

She jumped, heart in her throat.

It opened slowly, revealing DC Zak's cautious eyes, then DI Tee behind him, arms crossed, sharp gaze already slicing her apart.

"Lily," Zak said, voice low. "We need to talk."

She nodded, barely able to stand. But she did. She followed them into the interview room without resistance, without words.

They sat her down. Pushed the recorder button.

"We've recovered a USB," Tee said without preamble. "It belonged to Summer Millfield."

Lily's breath caught.

"We've heard parts of one of your sessions."

A long pause.

"Do you want to say anything before we begin?"

Lily looked between them. At their suspicion. Their exhaustion.

And she knew it didn't matter what she said.
Not yet.
So she leaned forward, her voice steady for the first time in hours.

"I want you to listen to all of it," she said. "Because Summer Millfield wasn't who you think she was."

Tee raised an eyebrow.

"She helped me. She made me feel seen. But she also *wanted* me broken. She *fed* it. Encouraged the anger. Told me no one else would ever understand unless I made them."

Zak's lips parted.

"She said I had to *show* people. That only pain speaks in a language people hear."

Tee frowned. "Are you saying she incited you to violence?"

Lily looked down at her hands. Pale. Still trembling.

"She didn't tell me to kill anyone," she whispered. "Not outright. But she pushed. She wanted something from me. And now she's dead. So maybe she got it."

Silence.

Then Zak leaned forward.

"There's more on that drive. Recordings. Files. We're going to verify everything. But, Lily—"

"I didn't kill them," she said.

She looked at both of them.

"And if you really want to know who did... then you better keep listening."

They didn't speak again for several minutes.

They just sat there, the tape running, the air thick with something unspoken.
The truth was coming.

But the truth had claws.

And it was still waiting to be unleashed.

37

DI Tee and DC Zak

The room smelled faintly of burnt coffee and stale paper, but no one noticed. The incident team at Westborough CID sat clustered around the central table, eyes fixed on the audio waveform bouncing across the screen. There was no chatter, no movement, just the slow, unrelenting voice of the dead woman they had once trusted.

"Some people become pain, Lily. Not out of malice. But simply because they stay too long. Like a wound that refuses to heal."

Summer Millfield's voice, rich and level, filled the space. It wasn't a therapist's voice anymore. It was something colder. The voice of someone who had already decided what the ending needed to be.

DC Zak stared at the screen, hands clenched into fists. The breath he exhaled felt sharp in his chest. "She's not trying to help. She's building a case. Justifying what she did."

"She's guiding Lily to believe the same," DI Tee said grimly, arms folded. Her jaw was tight, her eyes locked on the speakers. "It's not therapy. It's grooming."

Zak clicked to the next file.

A date appeared: Two days before Tom's death.

Summer again.

"You keep looking at him like he matters. He doesn't, Lily. You think your silence is mercy, but it's just avoidance. I did what had to be done with Sarah. And it hurt, yes, but that pain fades. Do you still feel it? Or are you starting to breathe again?"

Zak froze the playback. "She admitted it," he said, turning. "Right there. I did what had to be done with Sarah. That's not metaphor. That's confession."

Tee stepped closer. "We never had a clear motive. Sarah wasn't involved in the bullying. She even reported it once. And now we know it wasn't about Sarah at all. It was about Summer and her obsession with cleansing Lily's world."

Zak clicked to another file.

A recording labeled simply: Session: Private. Not to be shared.

Summer's voice again, but different this time. Not speaking to Lily. Speaking alone.

"I see it clearly now. Sarah didn't mean harm, but she stood as a reminder. A symbol of the world's failure to protect. And in that sense... she became part of the pain."

There was a pause. Then she continued, her voice softer.

"Tom was more direct. The kind of pain that echoes in footsteps behind you. I removed that too. But Lily... Lily is still fractured. The infection hasn't gone."

DI Tee looked at Zak sharply. "She's referring to Lily as an infection."

"She's laying the groundwork," Zak said slowly, horror creeping into his tone. "She was getting ready to kill Lily too."

The final recording shook the room. It was dated one week before Summer's death.

"Lily doesn't see it yet. But she will. Eventually, she'll thank me. When she's no longer waking up afraid. When the ache is finally gone. If I have to be the one to do it... then I will. I've always been willing to bleed for my patients."

Silence fell.

DC Zak sat back slowly in his chair, the tension visibly draining from his shoulders and leaving something far worse in its place defeat.

"We had her in our files as Sue Millfield, the top school-referred trauma therapist in the region. Everyone trusted her. Parents. Teachers. Even us."

Tee rubbed a hand over her face. "She used that trust to kill. To shape Lily into a weapon — and when it didn't work the way she planned, she aimed to destroy her too."

They'd already begun drafting the official statements. The public fallout would be huge. A trusted mental health professional manipulating a vulnerable teenager and orchestrating two murders. More, if she hadn't been stopped.

Zak stood. "We need to amend the file. Lily Shaw is no longer under suspicion for the deaths of Sarah or Tom, but she does still need to be psychologically examined, she did kill all of those cats."

Tee nodded. "Put it on the record. Summer Millfield acted alone. Lily was a manipulated minor. But…" She looked toward the cellblock, where Lily sat behind glass, alone and silent. "She's still carrying the weight."

Westborough Holding Facility — Interview Room 3

The light above buzzed intermittently. Lily sat hunched forward, her knees drawn to her chest. When DI Tee and DC Zak entered, she didn't look up.

She didn't cry. She didn't speak. Just stared at the floor with the kind of stillness that only comes after something shatters inside.

Tee sat across from her. "Lily… We know."

The girl's head turned slightly.

Zak set a folder gently on the table. "We've heard the tapes. All of them."

"She killed Sarah," Tee said quietly. "She killed Tom. Not you. Never you."

Lily flinched.

"She used you," Zak added. "She tried to make you believe your pain was your fault — that the only way to fix it was to remove the world around you."

Lily's voice was a whisper. "She always said… pain needed an answer."

"She lied," Tee said gently.

A silence stretched. And then, slowly, Lily looked up. Her eyes were rimmed red, but dry.

"She was going to kill me, wasn't she?"

Zak didn't answer immediately.

Tee nodded. "Yes. She believed the pain was you in the end. She'd already decided what needed to happen."

Lily gave a small, brittle laugh. "I thought she loved me."

"She wanted control," Zak said. "And when she couldn't have it… she planned to end you."

Lily nodded slowly. "I didn't kill them," she said at last. "But I wanted to. Sometimes. I hated myself for it."

Tee leaned forward. "You didn't act on it. You wrote it. You processed it. That's not a crime, Lily. That's survival."

Lily exhaled, her body seeming to deflate. "What happens to me now?"

"You'll be released into safeguarding care," Tee said. "You're not being charged. But we'll make sure you get the right help. Real help."

She hesitated.

"But Lily… your sister Emma she's missing. She's running."

Lily blinked. "What?"

Zak sighed. "She found the truth too late. And she made a choice. We need to find her not just because of what happened to Summer. But because she's not okay."

Lily sat still for a long moment.

Then whispered, "None of us are."

38

Emma

The rain had started around midnight, cold, light, and constant, the kind that seeped into clothes and bones, slowly chilling you from the inside out. Emma didn't have a plan. Only a backpack with a change of clothes, the hoodie Lily used to steal from her, and the bitter taste of Summer Millfield's last breath still stuck in her throat.

She hadn't meant to kill her.

She told herself that, over and over, as she ran.

But Summer was dead, and she had blood on her hands, literally. And metaphorically.

So now, she ran.

The roads outside the small town were mostly empty in the early morning hours. Streetlights flickered. The only sounds were the occasional drone of distant tyres, and the whisper of her soaked trainers slapping pavement. Her breath came in clouds.

She didn't have a phone. No money. No one left to trust.

But she knew one thing: she couldn't stay.

And she couldn't let the police write the ending.

A Country Road — 3:12 A.M.

Her thumb shook as she raised it into the wet air, every few minutes lit by the glare of passing headlights. Most cars ignored her. A few honked. One slowed, then sped up again.

Emma kept walking.

Eventually, a battered white van pulled over onto the shoulder. The driver was a woman in her late forties, in a neon parka with tired eyes and a strong Midlands accent.

"You alright, love? You shouldn't be out here."

Emma swallowed hard. "Just trying to get to Liverpool. My boyfriend's there. Got kicked out. I just need a lift. Please."

The woman squinted at her. "You got no coat."

Emma hugged her backpack tighter. "It got soaked. Please. Just as far as you're going."

The woman hesitated, then sighed. "Alright. But I drop off in Crewe. You sort yourself after that."

Emma nodded. "Thank you."

She climbed in.

Crewe Services — 5:17 A.M.

The woman handed Emma a half-eaten cereal bar and pointed her toward the train station.

"Don't do anything stupid," she warned. "Whatever's going on, just get help."

Emma smiled weakly. "Thanks again."

The sun hadn't risen yet. The platform gates were locked, but the fences were low. Emma waited until no one was around, then climbed over, hiding in the shadows behind an old vending machine. When the 6:01 to Liverpool rolled in, she darted onto the rear carriage.

She spent the entire journey pressed between a luggage rack and the bathroom door, holding her breath every time the conductor passed. She didn't belong. She didn't care.

Liverpool South Parkway — 7:44 A.M.

The train emptied. Emma slipped out among the crowds, moving fast and small. Her hood was up. Her clothes smelled of damp and metal. No one looked at her. She was invisible now.

Perfect.

She spent that day sleeping in the waiting room of a youth hostel, using the radiator to dry her socks. She didn't check in. Just stayed in the common area, nodded off, and left before anyone asked questions.

She was a ghost. And that suited her just fine.

That Night — An Alley Behind the Hostel

She crouched beside a rusted dumpster, clutching her knees, as flashes of Summer's final words played again and again in her mind:

"I did it. I killed Sarah. I killed Tom. But she—Lily—she was supposed to kill you. That was the plan... It was the only way to kill the pain."

Emma's stomach turned.

Everything she thought she knew about her sister, about what had happened... it cracked open like a wound.

Lily hadn't killed Sarah or Tom. But she had *planned* to kill Emma.

Summer had tried to turn them into weapons, turn Lily's hurt into something monstrous.

And maybe she had succeeded.

Emma stared up at the grey sky, her breath shaky.

The police would find the flash drive.

They would see the truth.

They would finally see Lily for what she was, not a victim, not a fragile soul crushed by cruelty, but someone *trained* in darkness. Someone who had practiced. Who had chosen silence over screams.

Someone who had once written Emma's name on a kill list.

And now, Emma had to vanish, not because she was guilty, but because she was the only one left telling the truth.

And no one ever believes the one who ran.

39

DI Tee and DC Zak

The flat was still heavy with the scent of blood.

Summer Millfield's body had been discovered just after dawn. DI Tee stood in the centre of the living room, hands on hips, eyes trained on the spatter patterns up the skirting boards. Quiet. Focused.

Zak moved through the hallway, lifting one evidence bag after another, scanning the scene for anything missed. There was no sign of a struggle, not really. Just one swift, decisive blow. It was personal. Messy. Emotional. And the vent, of course.

"The USB was left for us," he said, holding it up in the sealed bag. "No doubt. She wanted us to find it."

"They got her prints on the flash drive," Zak said "She left it deliberately."

They had watched the first file already. One of Lily's old counselling sessions, timestamped six months ago. Lily's voice. Cool. Clear. Calculated. A chilling description of her anger. Of helplessness morphing into control. And Summer's voice, calm and patient in response, drawing that darkness to the surface. Feeding it.

Tee had barely blinked through the recording. She'd just said: *"Play the next."*

Now, with Summer dead and Emma missing, the pieces were finally aligning, but the picture wasn't what anyone had expected.

"She's not running because she's guilty," Tee murmured, almost to herself. "She's running because she thinks she's the only one who knows the truth."

Zak exhaled slowly. "And she killed Summer Millfield because she thought no one would believe her."
Tee turned to face him. "Would they?"

He didn't answer, "All we know is, we need to arrest her for murder."

An Hour Later — Incident Room, St Cedars Division

The whiteboard had been cleared. Now it held three profiles: Sarah. Tom. Summer Millfield.

Below them: Lily Shaw. Emma Shaw.

Two sisters. One dead counsellor. A web of trauma, manipulation, and unfinished retribution.

Tee stood with arms folded, watching the timeline build again from scratch. Zak pulled up Emma's last confirmed locations.

"She didn't use cards. No phone. No log-ins," he said. "She's smart. Careful. But not trained. ANPR spotted her, in Liverpool."

"She wouldn't go far without a reason," Tee replied. "What's in Liverpool?"

Zak flicked through Summer's records. "That's where Summer was born. Changed her name from Summer Louise Millfield when she moved south, but it's all still there in old council records. Family, too. A sister. Deceased. No next of kin."

"She went to confront her," Tee murmured. "She found something. The USB proves she wanted us to know."

Zak leaned in, tapping a traffic cam image. "CCTV from a petrol station outside Crewe. White van. Driver ID'd her. Dropped her off around 5 a.m."

"And then?"

"We think she hopped a train. Unpaid. Hidden."

"Anyone check the Liverpool South CCTV?"

"Already requested," Zak said. "And there's more — the driver remembered she said she was meeting a boyfriend. Obviously a lie, but it tells us one thing—"

"She's thinking ahead," Tee said. "Buying herself cover."

Zak nodded. "But she's also exhausted, grieving, and now… hunted."

Later That Night — Temporary Command Post, Liverpool

Rain pelted the windows of the converted office space they'd set up as a staging area.

Zak sat hunched over maps and grids, coffee untouched beside him. "We've got unconfirmed sightings at two hostels. One staff member said she saw a girl matching Emma's description soaking wet, sleeping in the lounge."

"No ID?"

"None. Name she gave was 'Jessie' — could be coincidence. Or she's got just enough sense to use a false one."

Tee was scrolling through Emma's school records, re-reading her behavioural reports. "She's not a killer."

"No," Zak agreed. "But she is desperate. And desperation makes people reckless."

Tee's phone buzzed.

She answered, listened, then swore under her breath.

"What?"

"The second USB," she said, walking over. "There's more. Another tape. Lily. She's talking about Emma this time. About how she used to imagine what it would feel like... to be the last one standing."

Zak's stomach turned. "Jesus."

"It's not just fantasy," Tee muttered. "It's grooming. Summer was feeding that violence. Encouraging it. And now she's dead, and the only person who can confirm the whole truth is running scared."

40

Part one Emma

Emma kept moving. It had been four days since Liverpool. Four days of doorways, alleys, bridges, and shadows. The city that had once looked like salvation now felt like a cage. Every person she passed felt like a threat. Every patrol car made her blood freeze.

She didn't sleep anymore—not properly. She would close her eyes for a few minutes at a time, in hidden corners of the train station or behind industrial bins. Her body ached. Her throat was dry. And her mind—her mind was a minefield of guilt and flickering memories.

Summer's voice still lingered, cruel and seductive, even in death.

"She needed to destroy something to feel alive. You were supposed to be the last piece."

Emma wanted to forget what she'd done. She wanted to go back to before. But the blood wouldn't wash away. Her sister's face wouldn't leave her. And she knew, deep down, that there was no going back.

Still she had left the USB.

That mattered.

That meant something.

She clung to that hope as she slipped through another back alley in Wavertree, hood pulled low, hands buried in her pockets. She had thirty pounds left, stolen from Summer's kitchen drawer in the chaos. She used it only when she had no other option. A corner shop sandwich. A pay-as-you-go SIM card she hadn't dared activate.

She had no plan. No destination. Just a burning need for someone, anyone to finally see the truth.

And for Lily to know she hadn't abandoned her.

Not really.

Part Two
DI Tee and Zak

It was the CCTV that cracked it.

An officer flagged a blurry shot from a service station on the M62. A girl in a hoodie, face mostly obscured, hitching a ride. But the bag slung over her shoulder matched the description they had from earlier Emma's old green canvas rucksack. The one she'd taken on every school trip since Year 9.

The lorry driver had dropped her near Edge Hill.

They sent out a search grid. Local officers canvassed the area. But Zak knew Emma wouldn't be somewhere obvious.

She didn't trust anyone.
She was scared.

But she was also trying to be found, on her own terms.

It was a homeless man near the docks who finally gave them a lead. "You mean the girl with the hoodie? Think I saw her by the rail bridge. Didn't ask for anything, just kept walking like she didn't want to be seen."

They drove there in silence, the streets narrowing with each turn. Grey skies hung low over the Mersey. It had started to drizzle.

Zak spotted her first.

A hunched figure, shoulders stiff, moving slowly along the brick path near the bridge support. She looked small. Frightened.

But she wasn't running.

Not anymore.

"Emma!" Zak called out as they approached, not yelling, but enough to break the fog between them.

She stopped.

Didn't turn. Not at first.

Then, slowly, she did. Her face was pale, lips cracked. Her eyes held everything, fear, exhaustion, defiance. She didn't speak. She didn't need to.

Tee stepped forward. "Emma, we know what happened. We found the USB. We know Summer killed Sarah and Tom."

Emma's chin trembled. "Then you know I—" She stopped herself. Swallowed hard. "I tried to stop her."

"We know," Zak said. "But we need to bring you in. There are procedures. But you've helped us. You gave us the truth."

Emma shook her head. "It doesn't fix it. I still, what I did"

"It matters," Tee interrupted. "It matters that you told the truth."

For the first time in days, Emma let herself cry.

And this time, she didn't run.
Emma sagged with relief, but it didn't reach her eyes. "Then arrest me," she whispered.

They didn't put her in handcuffs. She walked willingly.

41

Emma in Custody

The walls of the interview room were off-white and windowless, but Emma barely noticed them anymore. Weeks had passed since her arrest. The trial had moved swiftly, Summer's confession on the USB had complicated everything, but it hadn't cleared her. A life had still been taken. The jury called it a crime of passion. The judge called it a tragedy.

Twelve years. With the possibility of parole at eight.

It didn't feel like justice. But it didn't feel like punishment either. Not exactly.

Emma sat with her hands folded on the table, her face pale, drawn. The sharp edges of who she had been—quick-witted, social, confident—were dulled now. Softened under the weight of everything she had lost.

DI Tee sat across from her, her presence calm, steady. DC Zak stood by the door, arms crossed, expression unreadable.

Zak leaned forward slightly. "Do you regret it? Killing Summer Millfield?"

Emma stared at the table for a long time before answering. Her voice was quiet, but there was no uncertainty in it. "Only that I didn't see it sooner. What she was. What Lily was becoming."

The silence that followed wasn't heavy, but reflective—like the pause between breaths.

Tee opened a folder. "We've listened to most of the recordings. There's one in particular we need you to hear. It confirms some of what you suspected."

Emma didn't ask which one.
She just closed her eyes and nodded.

Somewhere in her chest, she thought she felt something give—a crack in the wall of numbness. Not quite grief. Not quite relief. Something more complicated. Something like the truth finally landing.

And for the first time in a long time, she didn't try to push it away.

*

DI Tee and DC Zak

2:12 a.m. The precinct was dead quiet, save for the soft hum of the computer in front of Zak.

Most of the tapes on the USBs were already reviewed, catalogued. But one folder had been password-protected, hidden behind a line of code that even their digital forensics team missed at first.

Inside it was a single file.

SESSION 0 — Private Notes (Do Not Share)

He clicked. Static. Then a voice.

Not Summer's.

Lily's.

She didn't sound fractured or vulnerable.

She sounded *controlled.* Cold.

"Summer thought she found a broken girl. She didn't realise I was already rebuilding."

"Emma thinks she's the hero. She always did. But you don't get to call yourself a hero when you've spent your whole life standing by."

"I didn't kill Sarah. But I didn't stop it either."

Zak stared at the screen, then reached for his phone.

*

The lights flickered slightly in the evidence room as Tee paced in slow circles, phone pressed to her ear. Zak stood across from her, the recording playing again on the office speaker.

When it ended, the silence between them was heavier than before.

"We got this all wrong, she used her," Zak said. "Lily used Summer's trauma. Manipulated her. Fed her ideas."

Tee didn't speak for a moment. Her jaw was tight.

"We thought Summer pulled Lily into darkness," she finally said. "But Lily lit the path. And Summer followed."

Zak crossed to the board, eyeing the photos and timelines now warped by new meaning. "Lily didn't just survive the trauma. She weaponised it."

Tee looked at him. "And she used Emma as a shield."

They stood together in silence, two detectives staring at a map of chaos and grief finally seeing where the true heart of the storm had always been.

The Final Interview

The facility smelled of bleach and old plastic sterile, manufactured calm. Like grief scrubbed raw.

DI Tee and DC Zak were escorted down the corridor by a silent orderly, past reinforced doors and muted murmurs. The lights flickered with the slow rhythm of institutional decay. It was the kind of place where time didn't pass, it flattened.

At the end of the corridor sat Lily Shaw.

The walls around her were white and bare, the floor scuffed by years of patient shuffles and resistant feet. She looked perfectly at ease at the plain wooden table, posture relaxed, fingers laced together like she was waiting for a therapist to offer her a biscuit.

"Detectives," Lily said, as if greeting old friends. Her voice was light. Cordial. Almost amused.

Tee didn't return the greeting. She placed a small recorder on the table and hit **'play'**.

Lily's voice emerged, crackling from the machine:

"Summer thought she found a broken girl... but really, I found her. I knew what she wanted. I knew how to become what she'd keep protecting."

The recording played on Lily talking about Emma, the cats, the rehearsals, the almost-murder. Summer's validation. Her final undoing.

When it ended, the silence in the room deepened. Thickened.

Lily didn't blink. Didn't flinch. Her eyes stayed on Tee, curious, even entertained.

Tee leaned forward. "Do you deny saying that?"

Lily tilted her head. Smiled faintly. "Why would I? It's true."

Zak crossed his arms. "Did you plan all of this?"

Lily looked to him with pity, like a teacher correcting a child. "You can't plan pain, Detective. Pain just *is*. You either learn to live with it… or you make someone else carry it for you."

Her voice turned almost confessional. "I was surviving. Every day, I was surviving. No one saw that."

"You used Summer," Tee said, her voice cold and sharp.

"She offered herself," Lily replied. "She wanted someone to shape. To fix. I let her believe I needed fixing." A pause.

"I never wanted to kill a human. The cats were... manageable. Quiet. They let me *practice*. But Summer? She crossed lines. She got sloppy."

Tee's hand curled into a fist on the table.

"If she hadn't kept every recording," Lily went on, "you never would have found any of this. She was the loose thread. I was careful. But you were never looking in the right place anyway." Her lip curled, disdain showing for the first time. "It took you long enough."

Zak stepped forward, his voice low. "So what was the endgame? Was Emma always the target?"

Lily didn't answer immediately. Instead, she leaned in slowly, her voice dropping to a whisper, intimate and unnervingly calm. "She always saw herself as the sun. But I was the one living in orbit. She never noticed how dark it was. She never cared what the gravity did to me."

A breath.

"You always thought I was a shadow," Lily said, looking straight at Tee now. "But shadows know exactly where the light stands."

A flicker passed through her eyes pride. Triumph.

Tee stood abruptly. "We're done here."

Zak hesitated. "You really think you won?"

Lily sat back, folding her hands again. "Emma's in prison. Summer's dead. I'm getting the care I always needed. And everyone finally sees me. You tell me, Detective…"
She smiled.

"Who lost?"

The chill in the room sharpened. Zak felt it in the back of his neck, the prickling awareness that they weren't just looking at a troubled girl.

They were looking at someone who had *remade the world around her*—pain by pain, death by death—until she was at the centre of it.

And she didn't even have to lift the final knife.

As they walked back through the corridor, past the heavy doors and sedated voices, Tee whispered, "She's not insane."

Zak nodded grimly. "She's something worse."

42

The precinct was quieter than usual as evening settled in, the hum of fluorescent lights casting a soft glow over scattered files and empty desks. DI Tee sat back in her chair, exhaustion etched into the lines around her eyes, but there was a small, satisfied smile playing at her lips. After months of twists and turns, the nightmare was over.

DC Zak stood nearby, running a hand through his hair, a mixture of relief and disbelief settling over him. The file on his desk, now officially closed, was a testament to their persistence—a tangled mess of pain, deception, and darkness finally unraveled.

"Feels surreal, doesn't it?" Tee said, her voice warm as she looked over.

Zak nodded slowly. "Like we're finally breathing after holding it underwater for so long."

She chuckled softly. "I told you we'd get there. Took longer than I hoped, but we did."

Just then, the door opened and their Superintendent stepped in, a broad smile on his face. "Detective Constable Zak, Detective Inspector Tee. May I have a moment?"

Zak exchanged a glance with Tee, curiosity piqued. The Superintendent approached with an envelope in hand.

"First, congratulations on closing one of the toughest cases this department has seen in years," he said, nodding at the files stacked neatly on the desk. "Your tenacity, teamwork, and sharp instincts have made all the difference."

Zak felt his heart rate spike. He'd never been one for public recognition, but this felt different.

"Which brings me to the second point," the Superintendent continued, handing over the envelope. "I'm pleased to inform you that you, Zak, have been promoted to Detective Sergeant. Well deserved."

Tee's smile widened, and she clapped Zak on the back. "Look at you, DS Zak. That's huge."

Zak exhaled, a grin breaking through his fatigue. "Didn't see this coming. But I'm ready for it."

The room seemed to breathe a little easier, the weight of the case lifting as new possibilities took root.

Later, as they left the station together, the city lights flickered around them. Tee nudged Zak playfully. "Dinner? I think you've earned it."

Zak laughed, the sound lighter than it had been in months. "Only if you're buying."

They walked off into the night, two detectives bonded by a dark case but hopeful for a brighter tomorrow.

Epilogue

They buried Summer Millfield in a quiet plot at the edge of town. No service. No mourners. Just a headstone the council arranged, paid for with taxpayer funds and a line in a ledger no one would ever revisit. The plaque read *"Beloved Educator."* A lie few questioned.

Emma's trial lasted three days. The media called her *"the vigilante twin,"* painted her as both killer and victim, but the jury didn't see nuance. They saw blood, a weapon, and the body of a respected counsellor. She was convicted of manslaughter. Sentenced to seven years. Eligible for parole in four.

Her eyes stayed dead throughout. Not defiant—*resigned.*

She didn't fight the verdict. She barely spoke.

Lily never testified. The court psychiatrist declared her unfit. Too unstable. Too fractured. She remained in a secure psychiatric hospital just outside Lincoln, where she was studied, medicated, monitored—but never ignored again.

Sometimes, she painted. Mostly abstract shapes. Sometimes animals. Once, a red sun surrounded by shadows. The staff said she was calm, pleasant, cooperative. Her file said *high-risk with manipulative tendencies*. Visitors weren't allowed.

DC Zak transferred to the cyber unit six months later.

DI Tee stayed.

She still kept a copy of the flash drive. Not on record. Not logged in evidence. Just in a box at the back of her drawer, like a warning. Like a ghost.

Because even after everything, after all the answers and bodies and confessions, something about Lily still didn't feel finished.
Not really.

And sometimes, when Tee walked home at night—past the flickering lights and quiet windows—she caught the faintest whisper of a question that wouldn't leave her alone:

If Lily won... what exactly had they lost?

※

A plain envelope arrives at the facility under routine mail check.

It is addressed to:

Emma Shaw
Secure Facility D, Room 12

But Emma never opens it.

The guards return it to her locker, unread, just another piece of silence in the grey routine of her sentence. She lies awake that night, staring at the ceiling, the shape of her sister's voice pressing against her thoughts like fog against glass.

Meanwhile, across the city, Lily sits on a narrow bed beneath a reinforced window, humming a lullaby from their childhood. A soft, tuneless thing their mother used to sing when the lights flickered and storms knocked on the roof.

Her fingers rest lightly on the first page of a fresh, unmarked notebook.

She smiles softly. Almost lovingly.

And begins to write again.

"Dear Emma…"

The pencil scratches quietly as the page fills with small, deliberate letters. The guards will scan it. The therapists will read it. But none of them will truly understand what it means.

Lily isn't finished.

Not yet.

In her mind, the next chapter has already started, unfolding like a trap laid in velvet.

Because monsters don't always strike once.

And some stories don't end.

They evolve.

Printed in Dunstable, United Kingdom